a guided tour of ALLY'S WORLD

And coming soon, a whole new world...

Stella Etc.:

Find out more about ALLY'S WORLD at
WWW.KaRENMCCOMBie.COM

a guided tour of ALLY'S WORLD

MUNDUS

ALLYUS

KAREN McCOMBIE
WITH ILLUSTRATIONS BY SPIKE GERRELL

IMPORTANT!

Please observe the following
safety instructions before reading this book...

1. Make sure you are holding the book the right way up
(reading upside down can make your head go twisty).

2. Ensure fingers are free of toast crumbs and jam,
otherwise pages will get crunchy and may stick together.

3. Do not attempt to read this book when crossing busy roads.

4. Do not attempt to read this book when cycling, skateboarding, horse-riding
or sky-diving (pages may flutter in the wind and be hard to read).

5. Do not attempt to read this book underwater (unless you
are a trained scuba diver and have had the pages laminated).

6. Do not read aloud any excerpts of this book to people with no sense of humour.

7. Do not allow anyone except close friends to borrow this book.

8. Actually, tell close friends to buy their *own* book, just in
case they do not follow safety instruction numbers 2, 3, 4 and 5.
(Who wants a crunchy, sticky, crushed, windswept, soggy book handed back?)

Brought to you by the lovely people at...
Scholastic Children's Books,
Commonwealth House, 1–19 New Oxford Street,
London, WC1A 1NU, UK
a division of Scholastic Ltd
London ~ New York ~ Toronto ~ Sydney ~ Auckland
Mexico City ~ New Delhi ~ Hong Kong ~ Crouch End

First published in the UK by Scholastic Ltd, 2003

Text copyright © Karen McCombie, 2003
Illustrations copyright © Spike Gerrell, 2003

ISBN 0 439 98288 X
(weird but important numbers)

Printed and bound by Scandbook AB, Sweden

10 9 8 7 6 5 4 3 2 1
(more weird but important numbers)

FOR Ethan

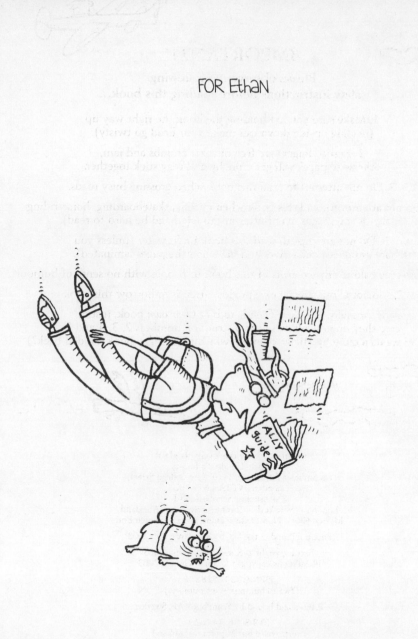

iNSide...

MY WORLD

MY FAMiLY

HOW WELL DO YOU KNOW ALLY'S WORLD...?

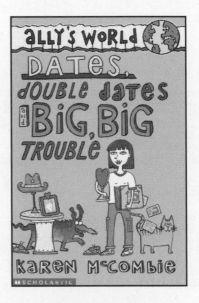

IN BOOK 1

Where do Ally, Rowan
and Linn lose Tor?

Is it

a. CAMDEN MARKET

b. ALBERT SQUARE MARKET

c. PORTOBELLO MARKET

IN BOOK 2

What hobby does
Ally's dad take up?

Is it

a. LIMBO DANCING

b. BELLY DANCING

c. LINE DANCING

MY WORLD

Want to Know about MY WORLD?

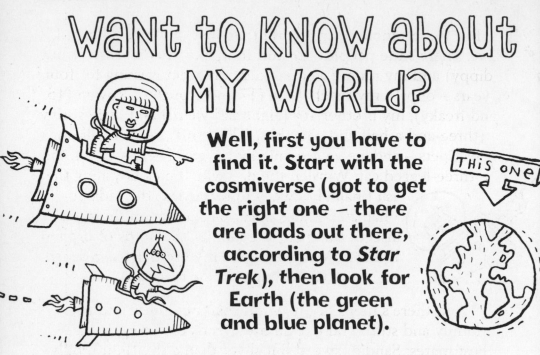

Well, first you have to find it. Start with the cosmiverse (got to get the right one – there are loads out there, according to *Star Trek*), then look for Earth (the green and blue planet).

THiS oNe

Next, find Canada (big place) – once you've sussed it out, turn right, and you'll eventually come to Britain (small place, compared to Canada, anyway). In the south-east corner of Britain, you'll see a big blob of buildings and roads with a wide river running through the middle of it, and that's London. Quite a way north of the river (the Thames) is a place called Crouch End (no sniggering at the back, I know it's a dumb-sounding name). In Crouch End, there is a street called Palace Heights Road, and in that road is a rickety old house with a cool attic bedroom that happens to be mine, all mine...

WHERE ? LoNDoN

UK

OK, so that's the geography lesson over.

But there's more to my world than just the house where I live. There's the people and stuff in it, like my dad (lovely but dippy) and my mum (who accidentally went missing for four years – oops!), my sisters Linn (17 and grouchy), Rowan (15 and freaky), my brother Tor (eight and weird) and little sis Ivy (three-and-a-half and adorable). The "stuff" includes all our reject pets – and we've got millions of 'em. There's Colin, the three-legged cat; Winslet, the dog who'll nick anything that isn't nailed down; and Mad Max, the sadistic hamster. That's not even *starting* on the stick insects, the mice, the rabbits, the herds of orphan buffalo or whatever else my brother has rescued and brought home recently.

And there's more to my world than my house and my family and stuff. There're all my friends too, like my three best mates: Sandie (sweet, but shyer than a shy thing), Billy (funny, but an idiot) and Kyra (entertaining, yet deeply annoying). Then there're all my second-division mates, who are… Actually I'll tell you all about them and their secrets later (page 70, to be precise.)

Another part of my world is the one that goes on inside my head. Some of the thoughts that whirl around in there are clever, some of them are interesting, and most of them are stupid, but I'm going to let them loose on you anyway, whether you like it or not.

So, if you want to know about me, my family, my friends, my school, my witterings on life, the universe etc., then you'd better start right here…

11

THE NOSEY QUESTIONNAIRE

☆ **Name:** Alexandra Love. (Ally for short. Or Ally Pally if Dad's the one shouting my name.)

☆ **Age:** 13.

☆ **Job:** Being Love Child No. 3.

☆ **My best feature is:** Um, I have nice toes, I guess. Kind of small and in a neat row.

☆ **My worst feature is:** Everything north of my toes.

☆ **My favourite colour is:** Sky blue. (Though looking out of my bedroom window it's pretty sky *grey* today.)

☆ **My favourite smell is:** Warm nachos, with gallons of melted cheese on top. (Mmm…)

☆ **My favourite food is:** See above.

☆ **If I was only allowed to eat three things for the rest of my life, what would they be?:**
1) Nachos (yes, I know I'm an addict and I know I need help).
2) Kettle crisps.
3) Crisps in general.

☆ **My favourite thing to touch is:** The fur on mystery furballs on my bed at night. (It's hard to tell which pet's which in the dark.)

☆ **My favourite sound is:** Waking up in the night and hearing mystery furballs purring or snurfling in the dark.

☆ **My best mate is:** Sandie (when I want a chat), Kyra (when I want a laugh) and Billy (when I want something to laugh *at*).

☆ **My favourite place is:** My attic bedroom, where I can stare at the view of Alexandra Palace in the distance. Or maybe the hill at Alexandra Palace, where I can stare at the view of my attic bedroom in the distance.

⭐ **My best subject at school is:**
English. And History. And I'm very, very good at Scarpering Quickly When The End-of-Day Bell Goes (I'm doing a GCSE in that).

⭐ **I have a talent for:**
Looking like I'm awake in Maths when I am actually sleeping with my eyes open.

⭐ **The talent I'd most like to have is:**
To be a dog-sled trainer. Then I could attach Rolf and Winslet to a sled and get them to take me to school every morning. But I guess that wouldn't work – with Rolf's long hairy legs and Winslet's short hairy legs, I'd just end up going around in circles…

⭐ **If aliens abducted me and said I could only take three things from my room to make me feel at home on their planet, they'd be:**
1) My cloud-covered duvet (it might be cold on Planet Tharg)
2) My Memory Box (I'm sure the Thargians would love to see my report card from Primary Three).
3) Whichever pets were in my room the night I got abducted (maybe all the animals on

Planet Tharg have three legs – Colin would fit right in!).

⭐ **Describe yourself in five words:**
OK, worrisome, funny, wittery, sane (most of the time).

⭐ **I'd cringe if anyone knew I…:**
Once ate Winslet's doggy biscuits just to annoy her after she nicked the toast off my plate. (She wasn't annoyed – just curious when I started making gagging noises straight after.)

⭐ **If I was invisible for a day I'd:**
Follow Alfie around. It would be bliss to stare at him uninterrupted, without panicking about being caught and blushing myself crimson.

⭐ **If I was a crisp, what flavour would I be?:**
Cool salsa nachos. Because I'm cool, of course. (Ha! I wish…)

⭐ **My motto is:**
Always have a bottle of ketchup handy when it's Rowan's turn to make tea (urgh).

☺ things that make me go **Whee!**
☹ things that make me go **BLee!**

☺ **Trainers.** The best invention in the history of inventions.

☹ **High heels.** Make me look like a constipated duck when I try to walk in them.

☺ **The smell of wet grass.**

☹ **The smell of wet dog.**

☺ **Cold pizza.** Shouldn't work, but it does.

☹ **Warm Coke.** Delicious as drinking a puddle.

☺ **Girls' Video Nights.** Your girl buddies, a table heaving with snacks, a great movie and some serious yakking. It doesn't get much better than that.

☹ **Boys invading Girls' Video Nights.** They snigger, interrupt, eat more than their fair share of crisps and make fun of you blubbing at the sad bits.

☺ **Pets.** They're just … funny.

☹ **Pet poo.** It's seriously not funny having to clear it up.

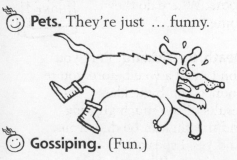

☺ **Gossiping.** (Fun.)

☹ **Being gossiped about.** (Depressing.)

Running fast downhill. Ace fun to do with friends, as you look like a nutter if you end up at the bottom of the hill collapsing with jelly legs and in a fit of giggles on your own.

Running fast downhill. When you're trying to catch up with one of your dogs, i.e. when it's trying to play with a rabid, deranged pitbull, or heading straight towards the biggest, blackest mudbath in north London.

Going to the movies. I like the trailers and the ads and the smell of popcorn and being in the dark. OK, and sometimes me and my friends like checking out the boys who are hanging around in the foyer too.

Listening to people eating popcorn with their mouths open when you go to the movies. Makes me want to chuck my cheese-covered nachos at them, that's how much it bugs me.

An unlimited, lifetime's supply of crisps. If only…

An unlimited, lifetime's supply of spots. Where do they come from…?

Death By Tickling. A favourite form of torture, as used by both my family and friends. Whether you're the one doing the tickling or being tickled, it's always a right laugh.

Death By Tickling. Pray you don't need a wee before you're pounced on by ticklers – the results of too much giggling and tickling can be disastrous. And yes, I speak from experience. (Shame!)

Waking up and then realizing you've got another whole hour to snoozle before the alarm goes off. Bliss.

Waking up and then realizing you forgot to set your alarm and you have exactly 43 seconds to get up/get dressed/get to school. Urgh.

YOU'RE LATE AGAIN

Rolf and/or Winslet staring at me with adoring eyes. Unconditional love is lovely, even if it *is* coming from a smelly-breathed dog.

Finding out that my new trainers/hairbrush/bus pass has been chewed to a pulp by Winslet, or buried in the garden by Rolf. Grrr.

Those times when my sisters Linn and Rowan are actually getting along. It may only happen for a few seconds every month, but boy, what a wonderful, peaceful few seconds.

Those times when my sisters Linn and Rowan are bickering. Still, foam earplugs are quite cheap and readily available from all chemists.

That first lick of ice-cream on a hot day. *Yum!* as it trickles down your throat.

That first rock-hard snowball landing on the back of your head in winter. *Yuck!* as it trickles down inside your collar.

Newly painted nails. Especially if I manage not to smudge them. (Miracle!)

Newly bitten nails. Especially when I regret doing it two seconds later.

Eating a whole bag of Maltesers in one go. See how many you can shove in your mouth at one time, then check out your bumpy cheeks in the mirror!

Sharing your one measly bag of Maltesers with your family. I think I live with a bunch of radar-eared bats, the way they can hear the distant rustle of me opening the bag, no matter how quiet I'm trying to be.

Beep

MALTESER RADAR

Laughing so much you can't breathe.

Laughing so much that snot shoots out of your nose.

Billy. He may be a berk, but he's *my* berk, so there.

PROPERTY of ALLY LOVE

Billy. When is he ever going to realize that burping in time to songs is not funny after the sixty-trillionth time? (It wasn't funny after the first time!)

BURP

Home. Of course.

Homework. Of course.

PIZZA BELLA

COLA

HOME WORK
A. LOVE

a guided tour of my ~~world~~ CROUCH END

Ever flicked through the back of an atlas to find places with really stupid names? Well, I guess Crouch End – where I live – counts as one of those stupid names. Still … home (stupidly named) sweet home!

A is for… Alexandra Palace; also known as Ally Pally (like me). Nobody royal ever lived there – the palace (and the park around it) was built in olden times for loads of mad exhibitions, like camel-racing, and re-enactments of Pompeii getting glooped by lava (with a cast of hundreds and loads of fireworks). Sadly, they only do stuff like the Knitting & Stitching show there now. (Snore…)

B is for… the Bench at Ally Pally, where I meet up with Billy. He once suggested that he carved our initials on it. I told him that if he tried it, I'd carve our initials on his forehead.

C is for… Clocktower. It's this big clocktower (duh!) on Crouch End Broadway. It's useful for a) meeting your mates beside and b) checking the time to see how late your mates are.

D is for… Deer. There's a sign at the deer enclosure at Ally Pally which says, "Please Don't Feed The Animals", but there's *always* some little kid poking Wotsits through the fence. This is very bad for the deer; if any little kids have Wotsits that they don't want, they should give them to me and I'll dispose of them, no problem. (Ahem…)

E is for… Elephants. Honestly, there were heaps of elephants paraded round Ally Pally during the time of the old-style exhibitions. Apparently, there was once an elephant swimming race there. Sounds super-cruel – hope the elephants sprayed all the spectators with water.

F **is for...** Famous people. They're the sort of familiar-looking people you see doing unglamorous things like buying Odour Eaters from Woolies and think, "Ooh, weren't they on telly the other night?".

G **is for...** Goat guy. He used to walk his goats along the nearby Parkland Walk when he went to the Unemployment Office. (Did he tie them up outside?) I don't know if it's true, but of course, Tor loves this story.

H **is for...** Highgate Woods. In the middle of Highgate Woods is a café that looks just like the house out of Hansel and Gretel. Luckily, there are no witches there, just really great cake.

i **is for...** Ice rink. There's a brilliant ice rink inside Ally Pally. At least it's brilliant if you can skate, which is something I am spectacularly lousy at. The old-time exhibition elephants would probably be better at skating than me.

J **is for...** Jelly, as in Hot Pepper Jelly, the name of a dinky, doll-size café near Crouch End Broadway. Honest, it is so weeny that when you're in there you feel

like Alice in Wonderland after she's eaten the cake that makes her huge.

K **is for...** KFC. OK, so more food. One time when we were in there, me and my mates bet Billy 50p that he couldn't eat an entire Family Bucket on his own. He won, but had to use the empty bucket for something else once we got outside and he started to feel queasy...

L is for... Lying on my back watching planes pass over. I've never been on a plane, which is why I love stretching out on the grass up by Ally Pally, daydreaming about where all the 747s are headed. And then Winslet spoils it by padding over and sitting on my head.

M is for... Muswell Hill. This area is on the other side of Ally Pally from Crouch End. Billy lives here, but don't let that put you off the place.

N is for... Nature reserve. A really pretty, wild bit of Ally Pally, with a pond full of bullrushes and a noticeboard that tells you about all the endangered birds and stuff that have been sighted there. Grandma calls this part of the park "messy".

O is for... Outdoor pool. Our local swimming pool has a cool outdoor lido. I can't believe Alfie worked there all last summer and Linn never told me. If I'd known, I'd have spent my entire holidays camped out there.

P is for... Priory Park. Me and Billy played a game of tennis there once, and Billy hit the ball so hard that it went right over the fence and *boing*ed off the roof of a passing ice-cream van. All the way home, we kept hearing the chime of "Yankee Doodle Went to Town" and were *sure* the ice-cream-van man was stalking us...

Q is for... Queen's Woods. Spooky. You can all too easily imagine a Victorian vampire hiding behind every tree. Well, you can if you're paranoid like me.

R is for... Rose window. This is a beautiful, *huuuggge* stained-glass window in the centre of Ally Pally. I stare at it when I'm waiting for Billy. I don't think Billy knows it exists.

S is for... Stanley. No – not Grandma's Stanley, or Stanley our dead goldfish. *This* Stanley was an eccentric Polish guy who became a local celeb when a TV programme filmed the inside of his house, which was stuffed with so much rubbish and junk that you couldn't get in it.

Sadly, he was very old and died, and I hope he wasn't horribly disappointed with heaven, which presumably would be a bit too neat and tidy for his tastes.

T **is for...** Town Hall Square. After school, kids from Highgate Woods School go along there to skateboard and check each other out. Me and Kyra went along one time, but this lad clipped Kyra's ankle with his skateboard and you'd think he'd murdered her, the amount of screaming she did (it didn't even leave a *bruise*). Didn't dare show my face around *there* again.

U **is for...** Um... (Think I might be a bit stuck with this one).

V **is for...** Victorian buildings. About a hundred years ago, Crouch End consisted of some grand manor houses and ... cows. Then all these Victorian builders went *splat*, and covered the fields in red-brick houses. Wonder where all the cows went? (Probably up to the exhibitions at Ally Pally to have races with the elephants...)

W **is for...** Wood Green. The high street is good for boy-spotting – you'll see 'em in Dixons drooling over PlayStations etc. or on their way to one of the two multiplex cinemas to watch something violent.

X, Y and Z... Look, there's nothing beginning with X, Y or Z in Crouch End (*or* where you live, I bet).

It only remains for me to thank you for taking this guided tour today. I hope you enjoyed your journey around Crouch End and come back to visit again soon...

THROUGH the KEY HOLE

PALACE HEIGHTS ROAD

LOVE 28

Welcome to my humble abode (and trust me, it *is* humble). This, in case you hadn't guessed, is the front of my house. Behold the neat front garden (ha!) and the immaculate exterior (double ha!).

And if we step through the front door, we will find ourselves in ... the **hall**. This is painted a delicate shade of lilac and is home to a fine collection of designer garments.

To our left is the **living room**, a light and attractive living space, streamlined for modern living, with a range of high-tech gadgetry.

Back out in the hall, we head to the **kitchen**, an informal family room, with many attractive, original features.

The kitchen opens up on to a delightful **back garden**, well-stocked with attractive plants, and boasting a useful shed and a much-loved child's swing.

Back inside, we continue upstairs, first taking a peek at the **bathroom**, with its striking colour scheme — red walls certainly show off the green of the plants to perfection!

There are five attractive bedrooms in this property, which we will cover in more detail later in this guide. But there is one additional useful space – a roomy **attic cupboard** between the two attic bedrooms. Currently used for storage, this has the potential to be converted into a handy office, or guest bedroom. Then again, maybe you should just shut the door and leave all the junk where it is…

A SNEAKY PEEK at ALLY'S ROOM

it's COSY, it's CLUTTERED and it's MINE, aLL MINE.

MAP

THIS IS WHERE I USED tO KEEP tRaCK OF MUM'S tRaVELS, MaRKING EVERY PLACE WE GOt a LEttER FROM WItH a COLOURED PIN. NOW tHat MUM IS BaCK HOME, I GUESS I COULD taKE It dOWN, BUt I LIKE tO LOOK at It aND PLaN WHERE I'LL JEt OFF tO IN tHE FUtURE. aND WHEN I'M REaLLY BORED, I USE tHE PINS tO MaKE StUPID SHaPES. LaSt WEEK, I MaDE a PIN PtERODaCtYL HOVER IN tHE MIDDLE OF tHE NORtH SEa. COOL.

desk

THIS IS WHERE I DO MY HOMEWORK. OR WHERE I SaY, "AaaRRRGGHHHH!!" WHEN I CaN't DO MY HOMEWORK.

TENNIS RaCQUET

I'M NOt tOO HOt at tENNIS, BUt tHIS IS VERY USEFUL FOR GEttING WINSLEt OUt FROM UNDER MY BED WHEN It'S tHE MIDDLE OF tHE NIGHt aND SHE'S CRUNCHING ON a CRUNCHY SOMEtHING aND KEEPING ME aWaKE.

SOFT TOYS

NOT ACTUALLY MINE: THEY HAVE MIGRATED FROM TOR'S ROOM AND HIS ENORMO COLLECTION OF SOFT TOYS. THEY ARRIVE IN THE NIGHT, ALONG WITH TOR AND HIS OCCASIONAL NIGHTMARES. THE ONLY NIGHTMARE I HAVE IS WHERE I'M GOING TO SLEEP WHEN MY BED HAS BEEN TAKEN OVER BY SMALL BOYS, TOYS AND SNORING CATS.

TOP VIEW

THAT'S ALEXANDRA PALACE, WHICH I'M NAMED AFTER. NOT THAT WE LOOK ALIKE OR ANYTHING.

MESS

GRANDMA TUTS WHEN SHE SEES MY ROOM THIS MESSY AND MUTTERS ABOUT IT BEING IMPOSSIBLE TO FIND ANYTHING. SHE IS WRONG. I KNOW WHERE EVERYTHING IS. IT IS ON THE FLOOR.

DUVET

MY DUVET COVER IS SKY-COLOURED, WITH CLOUDS FLOATING OVER IT (HIDDEN BY STUFF). I THINK IT'S EXCELLENT. LINN SAYS IT REMINDS HER OF MY BRAIN – VAST AND EMPTY WITH WISPS OF NOTHING TRAILING THROUGH IT.

Stuff and Nonsense

There's a place for everything in my room, even clutter and mess...

In the depths of my desk...
The top drawer contains: pencils (blunt); stapler (dangerous – once stapled my thumb to a geography project and created a new blood-coloured country off the coast of Peru); KitKat (valuable source of energy for rejuvenating brain cells shrivelled by homework).
The second drawer contains: an old hairy cushion that Colin likes to curl up on.
The third drawer contains: notebooks (featuring my family's stories); my inspiration journal; an emergency KitKat (in case I eat the one in the top drawer and then think, "Ooh... I really fancy another one!").

a) What's in the wardrobe?
Clothes, split into three distinct areas: Stuff I Like (jeans etc.); Stuff I Hate (school uniform); and Stuff I *Really* Hate ("nice" things that my grandma has bought me that I will never, *ever* wear, not even for a bet). At the bottom of my wardrobe is my Memory Box (see below), as well as a regurgitated furball in the corner that I haven't got round to cleaning up yet. (Blee!)

b) What's *on* the wardrobe?
Last time I was trampolining on my bed (as you do), I noticed a long-lost Converse trainer languishing up there. On closer inspection, I found a note stuffed inside saying "Ha, ha! Gotcha!" Something to do with my friend Kyra, maybe?

The mysteries in the Memory Box...

My Memory Box is full of the kind of family stuff that doesn't have a home anywhere else (other than the bin, maybe). After all, you can hardly fill a photo album with snaps of out-of-focus fuzzy faces, or huge black thumbs, can you? And call me mad, but I've kept this disintegrating Love Heart sweet

with the message "Fat Face" in an envelope for years, because it was the first gift I ever got from an admirer. OK, so I was eight and he was seven and we'd played together for five minutes on the swings at Priory Park, but so what?

Tor's first baby tooth used to be in there too, all wrapped up in a tiny box. That was until he showed it to Ivy, who held it very gently, examining it like it was a precious diamond, and then squealed "TicTac!" and fed it to Rolf.

The underworld... (be afraid, be *very* afraid)

Under my bed there is a forgotten world of dustballs and secret things. They're secret because I don't know what they are and didn't put them there – my insane, kleptomaniac dog Winslet did. Whenever I try to sneak a peek at what she's got stashed, she magically appears out of the gloom, chewing on a hairbrush/CD box/sock and growling softly.

In my murky make-up bag...

My make-up bag contains a rather exclusive range of make-up, called "Free Off The Cover of Various Magazines". All the top super-models use it, you know*. (*Er, not remotely true.) Useless contents include...

Black mascara – Makes me look like my eyes are being attacked by spiders when I wear it.

Blue mascara – Makes me look like my eyes are being attacked by spiders with hypothermia when I wear it.

Bubblegum-flavoured lip balm – Tastes great, but glues my lips together.

Purple glitter nail varnish – Sharp chunks of glitter that turn your fingernails into lethal, ninja weapons.

Black eyeliner pencil (blunt) – Felt very glamorous when I first tried it out, till Tor told me I looked like Cruella De Vil and then had a nightmare about me eating Dalmatian puppies.

Novelty nail transfers – Scratched an itch in class once and ended up with a sunflower transfer on the end of my nose for the next two hours, till Chloe and everyone finally let me in on what was giving them the giggles. (*Thanks*, guys.)

What are you Like?

Just tick the statements that most remind you of, er, you, and then all will be revealed opposite...

- ☐ I think I'm allergic to mess
- ☐ I can never stop talking, especially when I know I should shut up
- ☐ Why do people sometimes stare at me as if I've got two noses or something?
- ☐ Why do I get the feeling that people sometimes think I'm a dingbat?
- ☐ On Bad Hair Days I hibernate
- ☐ How come I always end up scruffy, even when I try to be smart?
- ☐ I play referee between my friends and family so often that someone should give me a whistle
- ☐ Pretty things always cheer me up
- ☐ Am I the only one who's not totally mad around here?
- ☐ I'm not grouchy, I'm just right
- ☐ Worry is my middle name (OK, it's not, but it should be)
- ☐ The best dreams are daydreams
- ☐ When I get nervous, I blurt out (lame) jokes
- ☐ I'd rather starve than eat curried macaroni cheese
- ☐ It's weird, but I'd feel naked without any jewellery on
- ☐ Me? Bossy?! Take that back, *now*!
- ☐ There are times when I just can't get my head around boys
- ☐ I'm not perfect but I'd like to be
- ☐ I like to be different (even if no one else appreciates that)
- ☐ You know, I'm sure that me and my family are from different planets
- ☐ A girl can never have too many pairs of shoes

If you ticked mostly 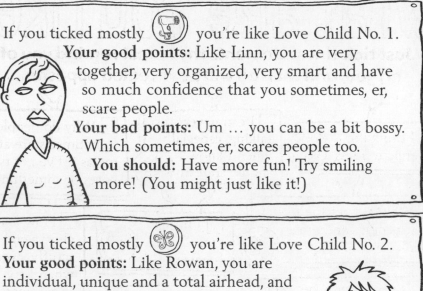 you're like Love Child No. 1.
Your good points: Like Linn, you are very together, very organized, very smart and have so much confidence that you sometimes, er, scare people.
Your bad points: Um … you can be a bit bossy. Which sometimes, er, scares people too.
You should: Have more fun! Try smiling more! (You might just like it!)

If you ticked mostly you're like Love Child No. 2.
Your good points: Like Rowan, you are individual, unique and a total airhead, and there's nothing wrong with that.
Your bad points: You're such a softie that your feelings can get squashed way too easily.
You should: Learn to stand up for yourself. Or just imagine horrible people on the loo (usually does the trick!).

If you ticked mostly you're like Love Child No. 3.
Your good points: Like Ally (i.e. me), you are friendly and funny…
Your bad points: …even though you're often so nervous that your insides would look like a wibbly-wobbly jelly if anyone had X-ray vision (which they don't).
You should: Tell people when you're feeling wibbly-wobbly, and not bottle it all up.

HOW WELL DO YOU KNOW ALLY'S WORLD...?

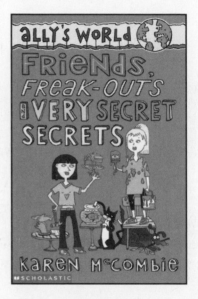

IN BOOK 3

Where does Ally
get a Saturday job?

Is it

a. A crisp-tasting factory

b. A card shop

c. A pet shop

IN BOOK 4

What do Ally and Sandie paint
on Sandie's bedroom walls?

Is it

a. Mutant daisies

b. Characters from
The Little Mermaid

c. "I love Limp Bizkit"

MY FAMILY

all about us

Here's my family, in order of height (as long as no one's standing on a box, of course...).

I'd work through all our (many) pets in the same way – starting with Rolf the lanky dog and working down to Brooklyn the baby stick insect – but we'd be here till a week on Tuesday and all die of boredom before then.

Y'know, I think I'm pretty lucky to have the family I've got, even if they are borderline crazy. Yeah, so Mum did vanish for a while (hey, that's another story) but she came back, and was as ditzy and lovely and hippy-ish and kind as we all remembered. Then there's Dad, who is a total sweetie and never annoying, except when he chases you around the kitchen with his hands covered in bike oil.

I get on brilliantly with all my sisters and my brother too. OK, OK, so I get on brilliantly with my sisters and brother *most* of the time. Sometimes Linn is so infuriatingly bossy that I feel like saluting at her, and Rowan can be such a maddeningly dippy airhead that I'm often convinced her head is stuffed with floaty balls of coloured cotton wool. Tor and Ivy are both so cute it's hard to ever get bugged by them, except when they tear around the house with Rolf, Winslet and Ben, acting like they're all a pack of demented wolf cubs. (All that scampering and barking makes it v difficult to concentrate on *Neighbours*. Er … my homework, I mean.)

Anyway, thought you might like a peek inside the family albums. You would? Oh good.

Linn's first glimpse of her baby sister Rowan. It was love at first sight. (Not....)

Rowan showing off her future "flair" for fashion. (By the way, I'm the bump!)

Dad playing "airplanes" with me. Me being travel sick.

Me, Linn and Rowan in Santa's grotto. Think Santa was quite glad to see us go.

Tor's first pet.

Self-portrait of Ivy.

This is Grandma and Stanley on their wedding day. Awww!

The Nosey Questionnaire

Name: Linn Love. OK, OK, OK … *Linnhe* Love. (But just don't tell anyone, all right?)

Age: 17.

Job: Being Love Child No. 1.

My best feature is: My hair, but only when it's straightened.

My worst feature is: My hair, when it's wavy and frizzy and icky. That and my stupid name.

My favourite colour is: White. Except every time I try to wear something white, some dumb animal gets a grubby pawprint on it.

My favourite smell is: White Musk perfume from The Body Shop.

My favourite food is: Anything that's not made by Rowan.

If I was only allowed to eat three things for the rest of my life, what would they be?:
1) Strawberry bio-yoghurt*.
2) Baby corn-on-the-cob*.
3) Hummus*.
*Except I'd never have any, 'cause it would vanish out of the fridge and be eaten by someone else, AS USUAL!!

My favourite thing to touch is: The white suede-effect cushions on the window seat in my room (my room, which I wish I could lock).

My favourite sound is: The click of the front door shutting when all of my mad family go out for a walk with our mad dogs, leaving me in peace.

(Apart from the cats and the menagerie in Tor and Ivy's room, but at least cats and stick insects and iguanas don't bark and yell.)

My best mate is: Alfie. (Ally, are you feeling all right? Why have you gone all flushed?)

My favourite place is: My room, with the door shut. (Ally, stop looking over my shoulder while I'm doing this. Make yourself useful and go and ask Dad if I can have a lock on my bedroom door, please. Tell him I'll appeal to the European Court of Human Rights if he doesn't let me.)

KEEP OUT
by ORDER
L·LOVE

My best subject at school is: Psychology. Which is why I know that my family is mad.

I have a talent for: Arguing with Rowan.

The talent I'd most like to have is: To have more patience with Rowan. (Fat chance.)

If aliens abducted me and said I could only take three things from my room to make me feel at home on their planet, they'd be:
1) Hairdryer.
2) Straightening irons.
3) Straightening serum.

Describe yourself in five words: Bored. Of. This. Stupid. Questionnaire.

I'd cringe if anyone knew I...: Was doing this stupid questionnaire.

If I was invisible for a day I'd: Be invisible (doh!).

If I was a crisp, what flavour would I be?: I'm not doing this any more, Ally.

My motto is: See above.

A SNEAKY PEEK at LiNN'S ROOM

THiS PLACE iS PRiSTiNE and PERFECT (NOT NATURAL, iS iT?)

dRESSiNG tABLE

LiNN KEEPS aLL HER NAiL VARNiSHES iN A NEAT, EASY-TO-ViEW ROW, GROUPED TOGETHER bY COLOUR. WHiCH MAKES iT VERY EASY FOR ME AND ROWAN TO SEE WHiCH ONE WE WANT TO "bORROW" WHEN LiNN'S NOT AROUND.

MYSTERY dRAWER

STRANGELY, THiS DRAWER DOESN'T SEEM TO SHUT PROPERLY – MAiNLY 'CAUSE iT LOOKS AS THOUGH UNKNOWN THiNGS MiGHT bE CRAMMED iN THERE. YiKES – COULD THiS bE LiNN'S SECRET, MESSY PLACE?!?

LiNN'S LOOKS

Apart from being bossy, Linn is good at other stuff, like being very pretty and very smart. When I say smart, I mean smart as in brains, AND smart as in the way she dresses. Oh, yes – Linn has lots of nice clothes. There's only one problem – can you spot it ⋆?

Linn dressed for her Saturday job.

Linn chilling out.

Linn out bowling with mates.

Linn going to the corner shop for a pint of milk.

Linn dressing to impress.

Linn taking the dogs for their last walk (i.e. pee) of the night.

⋆ I know! How can one girl have so many clothes that look identical? Weird!

LiNN'S MaTES

(yes, Miss Bossy-knickers *does* have some)

100% WONDERFULNESS ON LEGS!!

My sister claims to have perfect vision, but she must be telling porky pies. Otherwise, how is it possible that she has Alfie for a best mate, and has never, ever noticed that he is 100% wonderfulness on legs?! They met at an inter-school badminton tournament a few years ago; he came to her rescue after a whizzing shuttlecock got tangled in her hair. (What a hero!) Her other friends are Nadia and Mary, who look just like Linn. But as far as I know they don't cruelly boss their talented and wonderful younger sisters around. (Ahem…)

iN LiNN'S OWN WORdS (OR NOT)

I asked Linn if she'd like to write something for this guide. Her eyes widened, a smile of enthusiasm lit up her face, and she gasped, "Oh, yes, please!". Oops – wrong sister; that was Rowan. When I asked Linn, what she actually said was, "No".

Never one to give up, I asked if I could interview her instead. She seemed to think about it, and then said, "No". I persisted, but she still said "no", followed by, "Shut up" and, "Go away". So then I asked her if maybe she'd like to do a drawing or something in its place. Amazingly, she didn't say, "No" this time – she just grabbed the nearest pen and paper and came up with the masterpiece to your right. Er, you don't think that's meant to be me, do you?

Ho Ho

The Nosey Questionnaire

🦋 **Name:** Rowan Love.

🦋 **Age:** 15.

🦋 **Job:** Being Love Child No. 2.

🦋 **My best feature is:** My life-size ladybird tattoo. It's *sooo* sweet! (Even though Grandma nearly killed me for getting it done.)

🦋 **My worst feature is:** My knees. They're bony and knobbly. (If I stare at the left one with my eyes half-closed for too long it looks a bit like a profile of Robbie Williams pulling a funny face. Well, *I* think so.)

🦋 **My favourite colour is:** Raspberry. No – purple. No – silver. Wait, no… Oh, this question is too hard, Ally!

🦋 **My favourite smell is:** The jasmine growing in the back garden. It's *sooo* beautiful (except Chazza said he thought it smelt like wee last time he was round here).

🦋 **My favourite food is:** Sweet and sour bolognese. (I invented that!)

🦋 **If I was only allowed to eat three things for the rest of my life, what would they be?:**
1) Tuna and peanut butter sandwiches. (Mmm!)
2) Ben and Jerry's "Cherry Garcia" ice-cream. (Drool!)
3) Anything in the fridge with a "Do not touch! Property of Linn Love" sticker on it (that's always guaranteed to be yummy).

🦋 **My favourite thing to touch is:** The feathers on my pink feather boa.

My favourite sound is: Any of my CDs. They cheer me up when I'm blue, or make me dance round the room if I'm already happy.

My best mate is: Von and Chazza – I can't choose between them. They are so cool and amazing and inspirational and never make me feel like a kid, even though they are both three years older than me. And they understand me, which is more than you can say about anyone in my year at school…

My favourite place is: My room when it's dark and all the fairy lights are switched on. It's like a grotto!

My best subject at school is: Art, and ignoring people who tease me about how I look (drongos).

I have a talent for: Being creative.

The talent I'd most like to have is: Being able to ignore the drongos better.

If aliens abducted me and said I could only take three things from my room to make me feel at home on their planet, they'd be:
1) All my fairy lights (does that count as one item?).
2) My glitterball.
3) My blow-up green plastic chair (plus puncture-repair kit).

Describe yourself in five words: Artistic, sensitive, ditzy (Ally told me to write that one), sparkly, nice.

I'd cringe if anyone knew I…: Cried when I went to buy a pair of fuschia-pink velvet wedge shoes I'd been saving for and found the shop had sold out of my size.

If I was invisible for a day I'd: Do kiddie face-painting on all the uptight, narrow-minded, fun-free drongos at school. Can you imagine it when they caught sight of themselves in the mirror and saw a cute tiger looking back?

If I was a crisp, what flavour would I be?: A Quaver – floaty light!

My motto is: The world would be a happier place if everyone wore glitter.

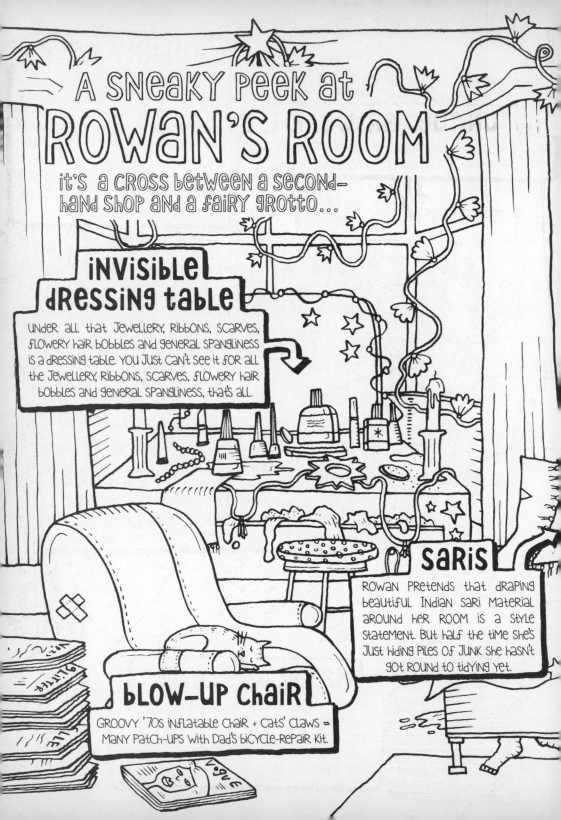

A SNEAKY PEEK at ROWAN'S ROOM

it's a cross between a second-hand shop and a fairy grotto...

iNVISIBLE dRESSING table

UNDER ALL that JEWELLERY, RiBBONS, SCARVES, FLOWERY hAiR BOBBLES and GENERAL SPANGLINESS is a DRESSING table. YOU JUST CAN'T SEE it FOR ALL the JEWELLERY, RiBBONS, SCARVES, FLOWERY hAiR BOBBLES and GENERAL SPANGLINESS, that's ALL.

SARIS

ROWAN PRETENDS that dRAPING beautiful INDIAN SARi MATERIAL AROUND hER ROOM iS a STYLE STATEMENT. BUT half the time SHE'S JUST hiding PILES OF JUNK SHE hASN'T GOT ROUND tO tidYiNG YET.

bLOW-UP ChaiR

GROOVY '70s iNFLATABLE ChaiR + CATS' CLAWS = MANY PATCH-UPS WiTH Dad's biCYCLE-REPAiR KiT.

"UNIQUE" ARTWORK

ROWAN HAS INHERITED HER ARTISTIC TALENT FROM MUM – i.e. SHE MAKES STUFF THAT IS "INTERESTING", "UNIQUE" AND, ER, "MAD".

JOHNNY DEPP

EVEN THOUGH ROWAN IS GOING OUT WITH ALFIE NOW, HER FRAMED PHOTO OF JOHNNY DEPP STILL HAS PRIDE OF PLACE ON THE WALL NEXT TO HER BED. THE WORRYING THING IS THAT IT'S A PHOTO OF JOHNNY DEPP IN THE MOVIE *Edward Scissorhands*. WHO ELSE BUT ROWAN COULD FALL FOR A GUY WHO LOOKS LIKE AN ANOREXIC ZOMBIE WITH LARGE KNIVES FOR FINGERS?

FAIRY LIGHTS

THEY TWINKLE, THEY SPARKLE, THEY'RE PROBABLY RESPONSIBLE FOR USING UP HALF THE ELECTRICITY SUPPLY IN OUR STREET.

MAGAZINE "TABLE"

SHE'S A MAGAZINE JUNKIE, MY SISTER, AND SHE CAN'T BEAR TO CHUCK 'EM OUT. SHE'S ALREADY GOT THIS PILE MASQUERADING AS A TABLE. WHAT NEXT? AN ARMCHAIR MADE OUT OF OLD *ELLE*s? (AT LEAST IT WOULDN'T DEFLATE LIKE SOME CHAIRS I COULD MENTION...)

ROWAN'S (GUEST) GUIDE TO LIFE

Hi – I'm Rowan Love. Names are important to everyone, of course, and I really like mine; the Rowan is a beautiful tree with lots of cheerful red berries on it that feed the little birdies [yeah, and are poisonous to people! – Ally] and Love means, er … love. But there are plenty of things in life that mean a lot to me. Here're just a few…

Having a bit of sparkle

When I was three, Mum lost me in this big old-fashioned store in Wood Green. After panicking for a few minutes, she heard some women "ooh"ing and "aah"ing, and spotted a cluster of shop assistants and customers gathered around something. Actually, it was a some*one* – it was me doing a twirl for my audience, dressed in a gold lurex top (it was size 18, so it felt like a ballgown to me), a pair of fluffy earmuffs, and a pair of huge platform sandals with pink suede flowers on them. I clearly remember Mum explaining to everyone that I'd "always had a bit of sparkle" about me, as she hurried me out of my new outfit and gave all the bits to the shop assistants to put back on the shelves. She mentioned my "sparkle" loads of times after that, but it wasn't till I was older that I realized she meant I was individual – and that's something I'm very proud to be. There's loads of different ways to describe people who are individual: "original", "imaginative", "unique"… and "weirdo" sometimes. Nine times out of ten, the person shouting "Weirdo!" at me is some brain-dead boy who's hanging out with his brain-dead mates, all wearing exactly the same crummy stuff. Thank you, but I'd rather be a weirdo with sparkle any day than be a dullsville, brain-dead clone.

Freaky friends

Unfortunately, in my year at school, there are loads of people with no sparkle at all, and to most of them, I am definitely the class weirdo. But it doesn't bother me too much, mainly 'cause I have got the best two friends ever: Von and Chazza. I met them when I was 14 and thought I was destined to be very individual, i.e. have zilch mates for the rest of my life. I was in this record shop in Crouch End one day, when Von and Chazza came over to me. When Von started talking I thought she must be speaking to someone behind me (well, she could have had a squint or anything). But she was talking to me – she asked me where I'd got my rucksack, 'cause it was really amazing. When I told her I'd customized it myself (I'd bought loads of old lady beaded necklaces out of charity shops and strung 'em across my bag), she and Chazza seemed well impressed. After that, we went for coffee and we ended up all best mates for ever, and I still don't believe my luck, because Von is stupidly cool and Chazza is in a band and everything, AND they didn't care that I was three years younger than them. People in my year at school would call Von and Chazza "freaks", but I say, hurrah for freaky friends – they rule!

The JOY OF GliTTeR

Ally says I'm addicted to anything that twinkles, and she's absolutely right. But there's absolutely nothing like something twinkly to make you smile when you're blue. And it works on other people too! Try this: dab face glitter on to your cheeks and kiss your mum, dad, dog and anyone you fancy. You'll leave a trail of sparkles wherever you go…

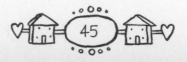

"These are a few of ~~my~~ Rowan's favourite things"

THE SOUND OF MUSIC It's a corny old film about a family with a million kids but I love it, and I love to sing along to every song (even though Ally tells me I always get the words wrong).

MY TATTOO Grandma was really against me having a tattoo, but even *she* thinks my ladybird is really cute. Hey, maybe next time it's her birthday, we could all club together and she could get one done too!

MY BRACELETS At the last count, I had 28 of these. Dad said he can hear me coming three streets away.

BELLY DANCING I go to belly-dancing classes with Von. It's one place where you can never wear too much spangly stuff. People there would think you were a weirdo if you didn't wear spangly stuff.

IVY Everyone in my family is brilliant*, but I've got a real soft spot for Ivy, mainly 'cause I'm well impressed by her fashion sense. Anyone who will only dress in pink is OK by me.

*Except Linn when she's in one of her Grouch Queen moods – which is, sadly, most of the time.

The Nosey Questionnaire

Name: Tor Love.

Age: Eight.

Job: Being Love Child No. 4.

My best feature is: My hair. It is sort of spiky, like a hedgehog.

My worst feature is: My legs. They are too short. Mum says they are the right size for when you are eight but I still wish they were taller.

My favourite colour is: Green. My iguana Kevin is green.

My favourite smell is: Fur. (You have to squash your nose in it. But it can tickle.)

My favourite food is: Noodles. You can make the best pictures with noodles.

If I was only allowed to eat three things for the rest of my life, what would they be?:
1) Noodles.
2) Mashed potatoes. (Good for looking like clouds.)
3) Toast. (You can cut it into lots of shapes. This morning I cut out a toast bat and I frightened Carmel in my class with it.)

My favourite thing to touch is: All animals. I like patting them all. Even scaly ones, or ones with bad breath and big teeth, I don't mind.

My favourite sound is: All the nocturnal animals who wake up at night in my room and squeak and talk and whirr round in their cages and mouse wheels and everything.

My best mate is: Freddie. Except when he is a pain and says stuff like my snail drawing looked like a picture of a poo.

My favourite place is: London Zoo. I would like to live there.

My best subject at school is: Animals. My teacher says that is not a proper subject. But that's not true 'cause Michael next door is my friend and a top vet so animals has to be a proper subject or he wouldn't have got exams to be a top vet.

I have a talent for: Talking to animals, but not using words and stuff.

The talent I'd most like to have is: To be a vet. (Duh! Stupid question, Ally!)

If aliens abducted me and said I could only take three things from my room to make me feel at home on their planet, they'd be:
1) All my animals.
2) All my books about animals.
3) All my soft toy animals (sorry, Ivy!).

Describe yourself in five words: I like animals a LOT.

I'd cringe if anyone knew I...: Once stood on a slug and killed it dead. It still makes sad.

If I was invisible for a day I'd: Do mean things to people who are mean to animals (like tie their shoelaces together without them realizing).

If I was a crisp, what flavour would I be?: Cheese and tomato sauce flavour (only they haven't invented it yet).

My motto is: Always worm your pets. (Unless your pet is a worm.)

animals a-go-go

These cages are full of things that go "eek!", "squeet!", and "nnneep!". There are hundreds of them, but TOR KNOWS every eeking, squeeting, nnneeping one of them by name.

KEVIN

BRIAN

MAD MAX

bookshelves

TOR has lots of books. They are all called things like *YOUR STICK INSECT AND YOU* and *CARING FOR SLUGS* OR whatever.

TOP AT CARING FOR ANIMALS
★ TOR LOVE ★

CARING FOR SLUGS

YOUR STICK INSECT AND YOU

posh certificate

...that MICHAEL the VET (AND OUR NEXT-DOOR NEIGHBOUR) MADE FOR TOR, TELLING the WORLD that TOR is OFFICIALLY TOP AT CARING FOR ANIMALS. I think getting it was TOR'S PROUDEST MOMENT. APART FROM WHEN ROLF CAME 2nd IN the LOCAL "DOG WITH THE MOST APPEALING EYES" COMPETITION.

A SNEAKY PEEK at TOR'S ROOM

STEP RIGHT INTO TOR'S ZOO-A-RAMA...

THE TIGER

DOLPHIN RESCUE

TOP bUNK

MUM AND DAD GOT THESE bUNK bEDS WHEN IT WAS DECIDED THAT IVY WOULD SHARE TOR'S ROOM. HE LOVES bEING UP SO HIGH – HE SAYS HE GETS A bETTER VIEW OF ALL HIS PETS. WE KEEP FINDING WINSLET SNOOZLING UP HERE – WE HAVE NO IDEA HOW SHE DOES IT. (ROPELADDER? FOLDAWAY TRAMPOLINE?!)

PHOTO OF STANLEY RIP

THIS IS A PHOTO OF STANLEY THE GOLDFISH IN HAPPIER DAYS, i.e. WHEN HE WAS ALIVE. ALTHOUGH IT WAS SOMETIMES HARD TO TELL IF HE WAS ALIVE – HE OFTEN JUST HOVERED MOTIONLESS bY HIS FERN FOR DAYS.

IVY

TOR'S TOP STUFF

The following has been brought to you by my very cool little brother. Over to you, Tor!

HELLO. MY NAME IS TOR AND I AM EIGHT (JUST). MY SISTER ALLY TOLD ME I COULD WRITE STUFF FOR HER BOOK. I WANTED TO WRITE ABOUT HOW YOU CAN TELL IF YOUR CAT HAS GOT A TAPEWORM, BUT ALLY SAID THAT WAS A VERY BAD IDEA. SO I HAVE DONE SOME LISTS OF THINGS THAT I LIKE INSTEAD. THANK YOU.

Tor's Top 10 Animals

1. Dolphin. Dolphins are beautiful and clever and talk in their own ~~compulcate~~ ~~compilcate~~ hard language.

1. Dog. Dogs are very clever too. My dogs know exactly when it is quarter to teatime.

1. Cat. Cats are very smart AND they can do gymnastics – they jump up on tables like they've got springs in their paws AND they are bendy and can fold themselves in half to lick the backs of their knees.

1. Slow Loris. You can see a Slow Loris at London Zoo. It is very, very cute – it hangs upside down and moves slowly like a sloth, but has big bushbaby eyes. I don't think there is such a thing as a Fast Loris.

1. Anteater. Their bodies are like a giant hedgehog and their heads are the same shape as a traffic cone. They have long tongues to hoover up ants with. They look very funny (but not to ants, I suppose).

1. Aardvark. Like an anteater crossed with a kangaroo. Cool.

1. Aye-Aye. These are a bit like bushbabies, but they have an extra long pointy finger and claw on their hand. They are way smart. They tap on bits of rotten wood, and bugs inside the tree think something is going on and start moving around. When the Aye-Aye hears them moving, it hooks them out of the wood with its long claw. Wow…

1. Elephant. Do elephants get colds? That would be lots of snot.

1. Mammoth. Like an elephant, only hairy. And extinct.

1. Small-eared Elephant Shrew. Not like an elephant at all – very small hopping thing that looks like a mouse on stilts. (Er, mouse-sized stilts – not people-sized stilts. That would be too weird.)

1. Bunny. I like their floppy ears.

(I'm sorry they're all at number 1 but I couldn't choose which ones were best.)

Tor's Top 10 Top Things To Do

1. Look at animals.
2. Look after animals.
3. Pat animals. (But not fish – they don't like to be patted.)
4. Watch animal programmes on TV.
5. Watch videos about animals.
6. Read books about animals.

Here is the News

7. Play with animals. (But not stick insects, because you could break them.)
8. Hang out with animals.
9. Go to London Zoo to see their animals. (They have more animals there than we have in our house!)
10. Talk to my friend Michael the vet about animals. It was him that told me how you find out if your cat's got tapeworm. You have to look at its bum, and if— [OK! Stop right there, Tor!! – Ally]

Tor's Top 5 Reasons To Be Quiet

1. Hide 'n' Seek. It wouldn't be a good game if you were noisy.
2. Not scaring little animals. Going "RAARRRGH!" at little animals can make them very frightened. You must whisper "Hellooo!" to them in a tiny voice and they like that much better.
3. Not scaring little kids. Babies don't like it if you go "RAARRRGH!" either. They get their own back on you by wailing louder than a fire engine.
4. People think you are invisible. I am so quiet in class that sometimes my teacher forgets I'm there. This is good when she is asking questions about sums and I don't know the answer.
5. Finding things out. My sisters act like I am invisible too. This is also good – it means they talk about stuff I'm not meant to know about and I find out lots!

The NOSEY qUESTIONNAIRE

❀ Name: **Ivy**

❀ Age: **3**

❀ Job: **ivy**

❀ My best feature is:

❀ My worst feature is:

❀ My favourite colour is:

❀ My favourite smell is:

❀ My favourite food is: **beeenz**

❀ If I was only allowed to eat three things for the rest of my life, what would they be?:
1) **Deeenz**
2)
3)

❀ My favourite thing to touch is: **beeens**

❀ My favourite sound is:

❀ My best mate is:

❀ My favourite place is:

❀ My best subject at school is:

❀ I have a talent for:

❀ The talent I'd most like to have is:

❀ If aliens abducted me and said I could only take three things from my room to make me feel at home on their planet, they'd be:

❀ Describe yourself in five words:

❀ I'd cringe if anyone knew I...:

❀ If I was invisible for a day I'd: **ivy ivy**

❀ If I was a crisp, what flavour would I be?:

❀ My motto is:

cat dug

A SNEAKY PEEK AT
IVY'S ROOM
A CUTE LITTLE CORNER FOR A CUTE LITTLE PERSON

MR PENGUIN
TOR'S FAVOURITE SOFT TOY, WHICH IS NOW IVY'S FAVOURITE SOFT TOY. SHE LIKES TO HUG HIM BY THE NECK.

PINK THINGS
IVY ONLY WEARS THINGS IN SHADES OF PINK. MAYBE SHE'S ALLERGIC TO OTHER COLOURS — MAYBE THEY BRING HER OUT IN SPOTS OR SOMETHING.

POSTCARD
THIS IS A PICTURE OF ST IVES, WHERE MUM AND IVY USED TO LIVE. YOU CAN SEE ALL THE CUTE SEASIDEY COTTAGES REALLY CLEARLY. OR YOU COULD IF IVY HADN'T DRAWN A HAPPY SMILEY FACE ALL OVER THE CARD IN RED CRAYON.

st.ives

TOY MOUNTAIN
IVY INHERITED THESE FROM TOR, 'CAUSE HE THOUGHT HE WAS GETTING TOO BIG FOR THEM. BUT SOME OF THEM STILL SEEM TO GO UP TO HIS BUNK FOR VISITS.

BEN
I NEVER KNEW DOGS COULD GRIN TILL I MET IVY'S DOG BEN.

IVY

The NoSey QuestioNNaiRe

🔧 **Name:** Martin and Melanie Love (er, Ally, this is Dad – I'll have to answer this on my own 'cause Ivy's gone and painted herself brown to match the dogs and Mum's busy trying to wash it all off).

🔧 **Age:** 40.

🔧 **Job:** Ace bicycle repairer.

🔧 **My best feature is:** Um, I guess I'm quite muscly and strong.

🔧 **My worst feature is:** I may be muscly and strong, but my kids say I'm as skinny as a whippet crossed with a beanpole.

🔧 **My favourite colour is:** Red – the colour of my very first bike, aged three (yes, Ally, I know that was a very, very long time ago).

🔧 **My favourite smell is:** Shower gel, when I'm trying to wash all the bike oil off me.

🔧 **My favourite food is:** Anything, when I'm hungry.

🔧 **If I was only allowed to eat three things for the rest of my life, what would they be?:**
1) Indian takeaway.
2) Chinese takeaway.
3) Pizza takeaway.

🔧 **My favourite thing to touch is:** A hot slice of pizza right before I magically make it disappear (into my mouth).

🔧 **My favourite sound is:** My family laughing.

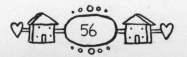

My best mate is: Your mum.

My favourite place is: 28 Palace Heights Road.

My best subject at school was: Getting into trouble for not wearing my uniform properly. (Won lots of super detention for that!)

I have a talent for: Fixing sick bikes.

The talent I'd most like to have is: To play guitar in a mega-successful band (I think that pays more than fixing sick bikes).

If aliens abducted me and said I could only take three things from my room to make me feel at home on their planet, they'd be:
1) Mum.
2) All of you kids. (I'd call you all in to the room first.)
3) My spacecraft-building manual so that I could knock one up and we could all return home when we got bored of our adventure.

Describe yourself in five words: Skinny, smiley, oily, happy, lucky.

I'd cringe if anyone knew I...: Sing very loudly (and badly) when I'm in the shop on my own.

If I was invisible for a day I'd: Run up to grumpy people on the street and tickle them.

If I was a crisp, what flavour would I be?: Ready salted. Plain and simple, like me.

My motto is: Always look on the bright side of life. And if you can't see it, put the light on.

A SNEAKY PEEK AT
MUM & DAD'S ROOM

it's a hippy-dippy heaven...

MUM'S SELF-PORTRAIT
YES, I KNOW it LOOKS LiKE SWiRLY bLObS iN a tUMbLE DRiER, but it iS SUPPOSED tO bE Of MY MUM.

MOBILE
MUM MaDE thiS OUt Of DRiftwOOD aND StONES aND SHELLS aND StUff that SHE fOUND ON thE bEaCH iN St iVES. SHE SaYS it REMiNDS HER Of thE SEa. thE CatS aRE VERY fOND Of it. thEY LiKE tO LEaP at it fROM thE wiNDOwSiLL aND CLiNG ON bY thE CLawS.

the bed
It'S VERY biG, whiCH iS USEfUL whEN SOME/aLL Of US (aND/OR PEtS) PiLE ON thERE ON SUNDaY MORNiNGS, LEaViNG VERY LittLE ROOM fOR MUM aND DaD.

spare bike bits
DaD OwNS aND RUNS a biKE wORK SHOP. bUt MYStERiOUSLY, bitS Of biKE SEEM tO fOLLOw HiM HOME fROM thERE aND taKE UP RESiDENCE iN thiS ROOM.

PSYChO CheeSePLANT

This cheeseplant has apparently mistaken Mum and Dad's room for Kew Gardens. I think there may be parrots in there somewhere.

NECKLaCe tRee

ALL MUM'S NECKLACES hANG fROM this VERY USEFUL NECKLACE TREE. IN ANOTHER LiFe, it USED tO hOLD MUGS DOWNSTAIRS IN THE KITCHEN.

CRYStaLS

These COMe IN aLL SORtS OF amaZING COLOURS aND ShaPeS, aND aRe SUPPOSED tO haVe SPOOKY heaLING qUaLitieS. I'M NOt SO SURe abOUt the heaLING thING, thOUGh   ONCe I dROPPed the biG bit OF qUaRtZ ON MY FOOt aND it LeFt a ReaLLY baD bRUISe.

MUM + DaD — hOW it aLL StaRted

Mum (aged 17) when she worked as a Saturday girl in a jeans shop.

Dad (aged 20) – Mr Rockabilly.

Mum and Dad's first date at a horror movie. (Mum was sick down Dad's trousers, she was so scared.)

Mum and Dad's wedding. The bunny fingers come courtesy of my uncle Joe.

ALL tOGetHeR NOW... AWWWW!!!!

The Nosey Questionnaire

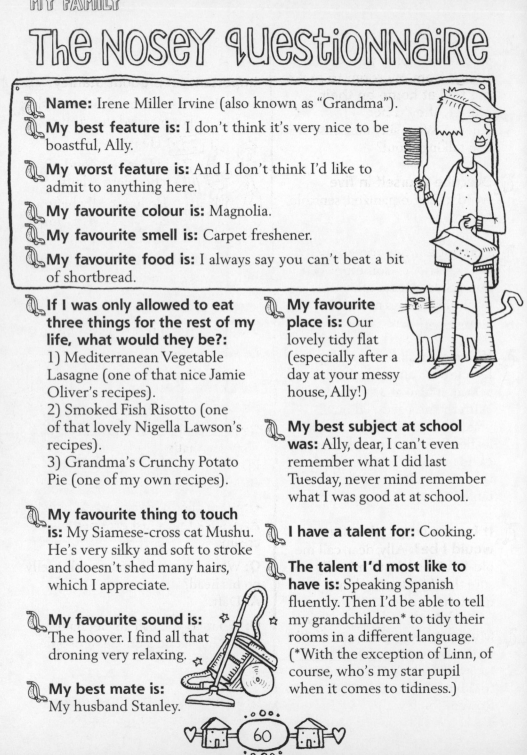

Name: Irene Miller Irvine (also known as "Grandma").

My best feature is: I don't think it's very nice to be boastful, Ally.

My worst feature is: And I don't think I'd like to admit to anything here.

My favourite colour is: Magnolia.

My favourite smell is: Carpet freshener.

My favourite food is: I always say you can't beat a bit of shortbread.

If I was only allowed to eat three things for the rest of my life, what would they be?:
1) Mediterranean Vegetable Lasagne (one of that nice Jamie Oliver's recipes).
2) Smoked Fish Risotto (one of that lovely Nigella Lawson's recipes).
3) Grandma's Crunchy Potato Pie (one of my own recipes).

My favourite thing to touch is: My Siamese-cross cat Mushu. He's very silky and soft to stroke and doesn't shed many hairs, which I appreciate.

My favourite sound is: The hoover. I find all that droning very relaxing.

My best mate is: My husband Stanley.

My favourite place is: Our lovely tidy flat (especially after a day at your messy house, Ally!)

My best subject at school was: Ally, dear, I can't even remember what I did last Tuesday, never mind remember what I was good at at school.

I have a talent for: Cooking.

The talent I'd most like to have is: Speaking Spanish fluently. Then I'd be able to tell my grandchildren* to tidy their rooms in a different language. (*With the exception of Linn, of course, who's my star pupil when it comes to tidiness.)

🐾 **If aliens abducted me and said I could only take three things from my room to make me feel at home on their planet, they'd be:**
Aliens?! What silly nonsense are you talking about?

🐾 **Describe yourself in five words:** Tidy, organized, sensible, fair, kind.

🐾 **I'd cringe if anyone knew I...:**
Oh... all right – sometimes I don't shoo Mushu off the bed, even though he's not really allowed on there.

🐾 **If I was invisible for a day I'd:**
De-clutter your entire house and get rid of it all at a car boot sale. With the proceeds, I'd buy vouchers for IKEA and some leaflets about their super range of tidy storage items and leave them to be found on the kitchen table.

🐾 **If I was a crisp, what flavour would I be?:** Ally, dear, call me old-fashioned, but I'm really not sure that I understand this question.

🐾 **My motto is:** Never put off till tomorrow what you can do today. (Especially when it comes to tidying bedrooms, Ally, Rowan, Tor, Ivy...)

STANLEY'S GUEST SPOT

Important facts about Stanley:

He is Grandma's husband (they got married this summer).

chocolate eclair

He is lovely.

He is very fond of chocolate eclairs.

He has scarily hairy ears. (I wish Tor would stop staring at them.)

He is quite silly. (I asked him to write something for this guide, and this is what he came up with...)

Stanley's (rotten joke) corner!

Q: What's black and white and very, very fast?
A: A penguin on a motorbike.

Q: What do you call a dinosaur that's hurt his foot?
A: Mytoesaresorerus.

Q: What goes "Quack, quack, oops!"
A: A duck that's just dropped his ice-cream.

Q: What d'you call a man with a jelly on his head?
A: Daft.

Q: What do you call an elephant who's just sat on a queue of people at a bus stop?
A: Comfy.

Q: What's green, furry and dizzy?
A: A gooseberry on the Waltzers.

PETS' CORNER

You may be aware that we have one or two (hundred) pets in our house. Here're some of them...

what goes on inside dogs' minds...

what COLIN would do if he had four legs...

He would try scuba-diving in the South Pacific.

He would learn how to jive.

He would go rock-climbing.

He would do catty cartwheels.

Cats that aren't Colin – at a glance!

FRANKIE
Distinguishing features: Bent tail.
Likes: Purring.
Dislikes: The hoover.

DEREK
Distinguishing features: Cross-eyed.
Likes: Sleeping belly-up by warm radiators.
Dislikes: Draughts.

Eddie
Distinguishing features: Fight-chewed ears.
Likes: Cuddling up to the soft toys in Tor's room.
Dislikes: Dirty litter-trays.

FLUFFY
Distinguishing features: Fluffy, no tail.
Likes: Tesco Wafer-Thin Turkey Slices.
Dislikes: Rustly plastic bags.

Tabitha
Distinguishing features: White furriness.
Likes: Visiting us. (She belongs to Michael and Harry next door.)
Dislikes: Our cats leaving nothing in their bowls for her to eat.

Of course, our family don't just have dogs and cats. But if I wrote about ALL the animals who live with us, it would take up the whole of this book, and since it's called *A Guided Tour of Ally's World* and not *A Very Lonnnngggg List of Pets*, I'll just mention a few.

MAD MAX the hamster
Likes: Tor, sunflower seeds, sharpening his fangs on the bars of his cage.
Dislikes: Everything else.

BRITNEY the pigeon
Likes: The tree in our garden, breadcrumbs, sitting on Ivy's head.
Dislikes: Her favourite branch blowing about in windy weather.

KEVIN the iguana
Likes: Sitting totally motionless.
Dislikes: Running marathons, salsa-dancing, skateboarding. (Probably.)

CILLA the rabbit
Likes: Lettuce, carrots, hopping.
Dislikes: Soggy lettuce, dogs barking at you when you're hopping.

BRIAN the stick insect
Likes: Hanging out on sticks.
Dislikes: Er … not hanging out on sticks.

SPOT THE DIFFERENCE!

**Can you find all the differences in these two pictures?
Whoever spots the most changes wins a prize*!**

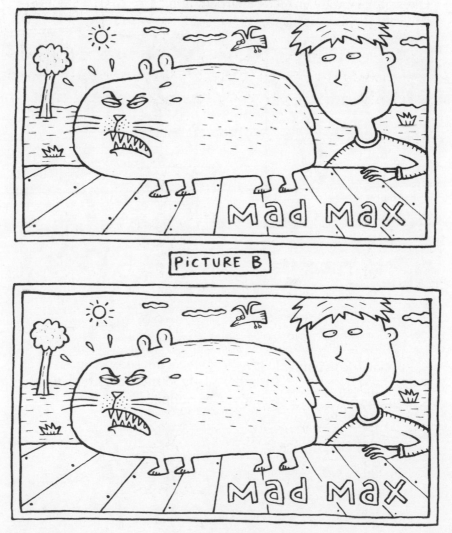

*Er, I might have been telling an eensy-weensy little lie, there. Sorry!

Answer: Tor is cross-eyed … and that's it!

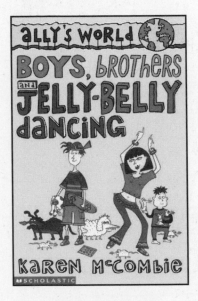

IN BOOK 5

Who do Billy and
his mates dress up as?

Is it

a. OASIS

b. The SPiCE GiRLS

C. The TWeeNies

IN BOOK 6

Which magazine is
Linn's boyfriend named after?

Is it

a. Q

b. FHM

C. J17

MY FRIENDS

MY TOP THREE MATES

You couldn't get three more different best friends than mine: one's sweet, one's dopey and one's just plain irritating...

Billy Stevenson

Officially my oldest friend. I don't mean he's 95 and uses a Zimmerframe or anything; I just mean we've been buddies since we started in playgroup together. Look – here's me and Billy mucking around, aged three.

Aged 3

Sandie Walker

I met Sandie in our first year at Palace Gates School. Back then she was called Sandra, was toe-curlingly shy and spoke in a squeak. She's still shy around the edges (and a little squeaky too, sometimes) but she's a lot more confident than she used to be. Just check out this school photo of us in Year Seven and you'll see what I mean.

aLLY

saNdie

Kyra Davies

I had the dubious pleasure of looking after Kyra when she started at our school earlier this year. Back then I thought she was a cheeky, obnoxious, pushy, know-it-all. Of course, we got to know each other and I eventually realized that she was a cheeky, obnoxious, pushy, know-it-all, who was also quite a good laugh. Why do I like her so much? Must have a screw loose, I suppose… Anyway, here's me and Kyra in the Hall of Mirrors at the fairground in the summer.

 Chloe and Co

These are my second-division mates. But don't tell them that in case it makes them feel hurt. What do you mean they'll read it anyway? Eeek!

CHLOE

Full name: Chloe Maria Theresa Brennan.

Best feature: Amazing red hair. (Only you must never, *ever* call it ginger, or she won't speak to you for a year.)

Is a good mate because: Her dad hires out videos from his shop and we always get to see new movies before everyone else does. Excellent.

Drives me bonkers because: Winding people up is one of her hobbies. Another one is laughing when you're annoyed at being wound up.

Most likely to say: Something sarcastic.

KELLiE

Full name: Kellie-Ann Vincent.

Best feature: Lovely, friendly smile.

Is a good mate because: She has bat-like ears and picks up loads of top-quality gossip.

Drives me bonkers because: She never wants to talk about anything serious. The school could be under attack from laser-toting aliens, and she'd still be yakking on about the latest soap star to have a boob job.

Most likely to say: "Hey! You'll never guess what *I* just heard!"

JEN

Full name: Jennifer Juniper Hudson.

Best feature: Cute upturned nose that crinkles when she grins (which is often).

Is a good mate because: She always gets the giggles, which are infectious.

Drives me bonkers because: She always gets the giggles, and then gives us the giggles, at highly inappropriate moments, like when our headteacher Mr Bashir is giving us all a stern talk in assembly on the importance of good behaviour. (Oops...)

Most likely to say: "Tee-hee-hee-hee-hee!!"

SALMA

Full name: Salma Hernandez.

Best feature: All-round, general, drop-dead gorgeousness. Grrr...

Is a good mate because: She tells it like it is. She is great when you want an honest opinion.

Drives me bonkers because: She tells it like it is – and sometimes too much honesty can knock your confidence a little. Make that a *lot*.

Most likely to say: "Your top is really, really nice! The one you had on yesterday was the pits, though."

top mate tips

OK, so I'm no expert, but here's how I think the Best Mate Rules should look...

1. Never put each other down. Teasing is one thing, but you should always know where to draw the line. (Are you listening, Kyra and Chloe, o, sarcastic chums of mine?)

2. Always tell each other the truth. A true friend is someone who won't let you walk around school with a bit of loo paper stuck to the heel of your shoe. (Kyra and Chloe, are you listening again?!)

3. Always know when to use a white lie. "I just don't think the colour's right" is much kinder than "Jen, you look like a sheep with boobs in that jumper".

4. Be generous. Lending her that top she likes so much means you're a truly kind and wonderful human being. And it also means she's more likely to lend *you* her new CD. (Unless you're Kellie, who's got the worst taste in CDs you've ever seen – you seriously *don't* want to borrow her stuff...)

5. Don't take advantage of her. If you end up borrowing every *one* of her CDs and never bothering to buy your own, that makes you a) mean, and b) a friend-free, music-free zone very shortly. Hmm, you know, I've just realized Billy has half my CD collection...

6. Never exclude each other. Boys, other mates, hobbies ... all of them can clutter up your life (in the nicest possible way). But while you're busy drooling over a boyfriend/hanging out with new mates/learning trapeze or whatever, don't neglect your best buddy.

7. Make each other giggle.

She's down because her parents are fighting/her baby sister covered her brand new boots in baby puke/the boy she fancies is as interested in her as measles. As a best friend, it's your business to get her grinning again. (For me and my friends, Death By Tickling usually works – see page 15.)

8. Share your crisps/Maltesers/tub of Häagen-Dazs.

There's nothing that proves loyalty more than sharing your favourite munchies. (Yes, you *can* have my last Quaver, Salma, even though you just finished off those Hula Hoops all on your *own*, I notice…)

HOW TO ALWAYS SAY EXACTLY THE RIGHT THING

Has your mate got parent problems? Boyfriend blues? Teacher trouble? Clothes crisis? Whatever's going on in her life, as she babbles away, lift your finger then drop it on the pie chart below, and – hey presto! – you'll say exactly the right thing to cheer her up. (Er, eventually…)

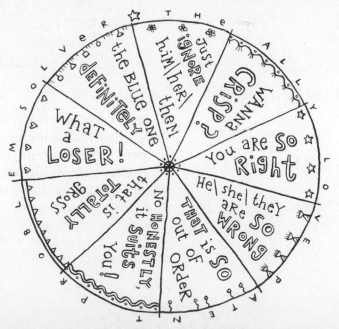

the LOUSY fRiENdS CLUb

**Got a mate who's a member?
After extensive research (i.e. remembering all
the lousy friends I've come across in the past)
here's how to tell...**

The BOSSY-BOOtS

Aleesha (Sixer in my Brownie pack) loved to tell me what to do and think every second I was in her company, and didn't realize that I had a fully functioning brain and could make decisions for myself. Actually, the Bossy-Boots, like Aleesha, isn't in the least bit interested in what you've got inside your head, just as long as you nod it a lot when she's bossing you about.

The PRiNCeSS

Miranda (in my Primary Six class) dished out sugar-coated insults – i.e. she took one look at me after I got my hair cut, smiled sweetly and said, "Wow! You look almost pretty now!". OK, so maybe, as a type, the Princess is a tiny bit prettier/trendier/cleverer/whateverer than you, but does she have to (ever-so-slightly) rub your nose in it? Yes, 'cause it makes her feel superior.

The SPONGE

Briony (my friend for the first month when I started at Palace Gates School) used me as her unpaid analyst, expecting me to talk over her every woe for ever. I didn't mind commiserating with her over her dead budgie or her favourite TV series ending or whatever, till I realized that my house could have been crushed in a freak tornado and she wouldn't have a clue about it, she was so wrapped up in herself.

The MAGPIE

She can't help herself; she's got a perfectly nice life of her own, but she keeps trying to nick bits of yours. You know the feeling: your bedroom starts to look strangely minimalist, while you get a sense of déjà vu when you're in hers – mainly 'cause most of your stuff has magically migrated to Miss Magpie's bedroom. (Actually the half of my CD collection that Billy doesn't have is currently round at Kyra's, along with my black cords, my geography notes and a pile of *Sugar* magazines I lent her about a century ago...)

WARNING!

If any of the above sounds like one of your friends, then it's time to stand up for yourself and ... sack them. Go on – it's for the good of your health! (And yes, I know it makes you feel like a total creepoid in the meantime...)

Excellent things to do with mates

Boys and families are banned – there're times when only the girlies will do!

Girls' Video Nights

Who needs boys interrupting a great slushy movie by moaning about the hero's duff hairdo and the heroine's general wimpiness? OK – us girls know that stuff too, but we're willing to suspend our disbelief and have fun eating popcorn till we're nearly sick and passing tissues to anyone who's got leaky eyes. (Why don't boys get that?!)

TOP SLUSHY Video

POP CORN

zzzzz

Pizza Bella

Sleepovers

If you were on your own, the idea of sleeping on hard floorboards with only a millimetre of fabric to cushion your bones would sound insane. But do it with a bunch of mates, loads of food, a tonne of gossip and some stupid pyjamas and it seems like the best idea since takeaway pizzas.

Shopping

Trying on drop-dead gorgeous clothes and doing a spin in front of your approving friends: fun. Trying on terrible clothes and doing a spin in front of your friends who can't quite get breath they're laughing so much: ace fun.

Dress rehearsals

This is a pre-going-out-somewhere-special ritual that me and my friends always do. It's a bit like shopping, only you're in someone's bedroom, so you can be a lot louder and sillier and try on seventy-five different outfits without a sales assistant wandering in and giving you the evil eye. Although the odd passing parent might tut and shake their head...

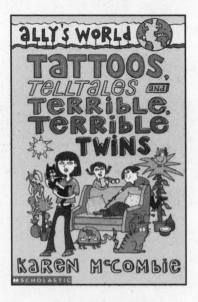

IN BOOK 7

What breed is Kyra's kitten, Mushu?

Is it

a. PART-BURMESE

b. PART-PEKINESE

c. PART-SIAMESE

IN BOOK 8

What does Rowan get a tattoo of?

Is it

a. A LADYBIRD

b. AN EARWIG

c. A BUMBLEBEE

SCHOOL STUFF

Palace
gates

A. LOVE

Teachers at a Glance

Here are five of my teachers, in the outfits they wore for a charity do at our school – 'cause in their normal clothes, they'd be way too boring to look at.

Explanation of symbols

 Surprisingly human and nice

 Makes subject interesting

 Boring

 Very boring

 Hates pupils with a vengeance

 Shouts too much

 Has bad breath

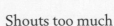 Has sense of humour bypass

Miss Thomson (History)

Lovely. Never makes you feel guilty or brain-dead if you don't know the answer to a question. Wears perfume that smells like a cross between cinnamon and fabric conditioner.

Mr Samuels (English)

Can be OK, but sometimes turns into Mr Shouty-Angry; i.e. when boys in class are messing about and sticking pencils up their noses instead of being riveted by Shakespeare's sonnets.

Mr Horace (Maths)

Should have been an accountant. Or a lorry driver. Or a stuntman. Basically, he should have been anything but a maths teacher, since it is blindingly obvious that he really, truly hates his job.

Miss Kyriacou (Science)

Waffles a lot when trying to explain stuff, which makes difficult subjects even more difficult to understand. Squeezes herself into clothes nearly two sizes too small. (Not a pretty sight.)

Mr Matthews (French)

Once swore in French by accident, but then refused to tell us what it meant. (Boo.) Breath smells of garlic and dog food, weirdly. Wonder what "breath freshener" is in French?

Want to know what Palace Gates school is like? Welcome to my version of...

OPEN DAY

SCHOOL UNIFORM

Some schools round Crouch End don't make you wear school uniform. Sadly, ours does (boo), unless you're in sixth form. This is cruel and unjust, as you can plainly see.

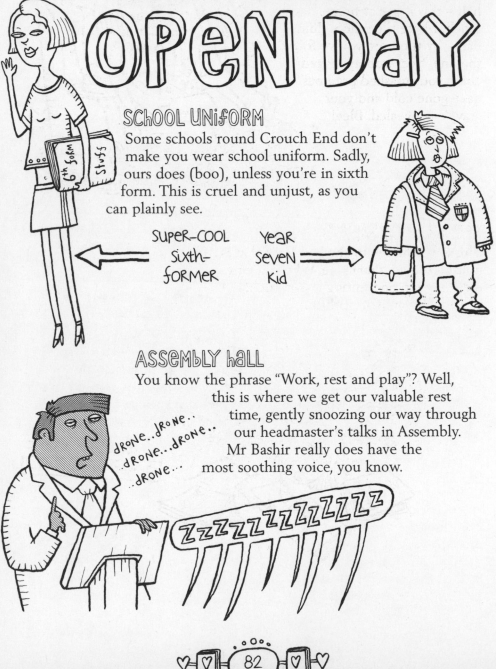

← SUPER-COOL SIXTH-FORMER

YEAR SEVEN KID →

ASSEMBLY HALL

You know the phrase "Work, rest and play"? Well, this is where we get our valuable rest time, gently snoozing our way through our headmaster's talks in Assembly. Mr Bashir really does have the most soothing voice, you know.

drone..drone.. drone...drone.. ..drone...

ZZZZZZZZZZZZZ

The dinner hall

Um, OK … so this isn't the dinner hall – this is me at home, having lunch. I hate the school dinner hall – by the time you've found the one, free, wobbly-legged chair, your mashed potatoes have gone cold and your gravy's congealed. Blee!

The hall of shame

This is the hall with the lino floor that is polished to a lethal shine. Why, oh, why did I have to be wearing a skirt the day I went flying on it? Arghhhh…

MOMENT OF SHAME
ACTION REPLAY..

SCHOOL STUFF

The Girls' Loos

In here you will find girls gossiping, putting on make-up, reading magazines, giggling, sobbing and – occasionally – going for a wee. Note: in the second cubicle on the right is a life-like drawing of our "much-missed" year head Mrs Fisher, who has "sadly" gone to another school.

The Boys' Loos

You must rush past here very, very fast, holding your breath. (Why do boys' loos always smell like a load of tramps just died in there?)

do you have a short attention span?

Well, do you? Or have you fallen asleep already?!

1. Concentrating in class can be very difficult when…
A) Your mind is trying to process such a lot of fascinating information.
B) Your mate is babbling about *Hollyoaks* in your ear.
C) Your eyelids feel like they weigh three kilos each.

2. The teacher has just said something. What was it?
A) "Open your books at page 71."
B) "Do you like my nail varnish?" Oh no – that was your mate.
C) Um … "Blah, blah, blah"?

3. The teacher has just told you what your homework assignment is. What has the teacher just told you?
A) What our homework assignment is! Duh!
B) Sorry – you missed that 'cause your mate was just showing you her belly-button piercing that's gone septic.
C) What?

4. There is a test paper in front of you. You are thinking…
A) "Hmm – looks tough, but I think I can do it."
B) "That belly-button piercing looked gross!"
C) "What will I have for tea tonight…?"

5. You have your hand up in class. This is because…
A) You know the answer to the question.
B) You need to go to the loo.
C) Um … you can't remember.

Scores (or snores…)
If you answered mostly
As – You could get an A-level in attentiveness. If there is such a word. Your name is probably Linn. (Swot…)
Bs – You could do with moving to a seat next to a non-blabbermouth. Your name is probably Ally. (And you're probably sitting next to Kyra.)
Cs – You need to concentrate much much harder, and maybe get some more sleep too. No – not right now! Your name is probably Billy.

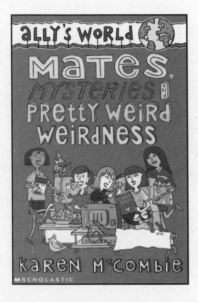

IN BOOK 9

What does Tor
call poltergeists?

Is it

a. POLTERGEESE

b. POLTERGHOSTS

C. POLTERGNOMES

IN BOOK 10

What does Grandma say Ally,
Rowan and Linn's bridesmaid's
outfits have to be?

Is it

a. PASTEL

b. PLAID

C. PVC

BOY BiT

YOU boYS aRe WeiRD

Don't go off in a huff, Billy – this is about *all* boys, not just you. (Although a lot of this does sound spookily like you, now I come to think of it...)

- You think that goofing around like a hyperactive orang-utan will make us fancy you. You are *so* wrong.

- Your rooms smell like hamster cages. What's that all about?

- You can have a two-hour conversation with someone and then act like you never spoke a word to each other. ("So, what was Hassan saying, Billy?" "Erm, not much." "Well, what's he up to?" "Uh … dunno.")

- If something is stuck or not working properly, you think that hitting it hard will help. It won't. Whatever you've hit will just break, or stay stuck. (Hey, Billy – remember that time you did a kick-box move on your jammed back-garden gate and your foot went straight through the rotten wood? Just as well your mum found that hacksaw to cut you free, wasn't it?!)

- You show your friends that you like them by punching them hard on the arm, calling them offensive names and getting them in a headlock.

- Your daily grooming routine involves: having a shower; thinking about brushing your teeth but then not bothering; slapping your hair a few times till it stops sticking up OR ruffling your fingers through till it *does* stick up; picking your nose and studying whatever you find wedged up there. (*Yes*, Billy – don't think I haven't noticed!)

Yeah? Well, you Girls are Weird

Who's in a huff, Ally? Everyone knows that boys are great and girls are from the Planet Paranoid...

• You think we goof around to impress you. Ha! We're just goofing around for the total fun of goofing around.

• In your rooms you stash a tonne of deodorant, body spray, perfume, scented bath oil and pongy aromatherapy stuff. What for? Do you all smell really bad?

• You can have a two-hour conversation with someone and find out the most mind-numbingly dull facts about them. (Who cares if Jen's sister got a new hairdryer for five quid off in a sale at Comet, Ally? *Snorrrre*...)

• If something is stuck or not working properly, you cry. (Yeah, like *that*'s going to fix it!)

• You show your friends that you like them by hugging them and stuff, like you haven't seen them for four hundred years, instead of just yesterday, when you were round their house watching soppy videos.

• Your daily grooming routine involves: having a shower; brushing your teeth; staring in the mirror moaning about how your hair looks funny; staring in the mirror moaning about how you've got some invisible spot on your chin; squeezing the invisible spot on your chin till it turns into a throbbing great red boil; staring into every mirror/window/reflective surface for the whole day moaning about your boil and your funny hair. (Yeah, I clocked you, Ally!)

10 ways to get that guy!

Before someone yelps, "But Ally, you know less than nothing about getting guys!", this page comes courtesy of my man-eating mate Kyra (who else?).

EXPERT

1. "Walk a dog past his house fourteen times a day in the hope of running into him. If you don't have a dog, borrow one."

[Yeah, a cat or a hamster would just look suspicious – Ally]

2. "Find out what his hobbies are and take them up too."
[Hmm... not a great idea if he's into car-jacking, taxidermy or yodelling – Ally]

3. "Pay him a compliment, This should be something like, 'You scored a great goal the other day' and not something wet like 'the way you hold your pencil is nice'."

4. "Make sure you always look your best when you're around him."
[i.e. check you don't have your skirt tucked into your knickers – Ally]

5. "Find out his star sign, swot up about it, then impress him with your knowledge. But this can be tricky, 'cause while most boys can tell you the name of every character in *Star Wars*, they often haven't a clue what their own star sign is."

CAPRICORNICUS

[Very true. I once asked Billy what his was and he said, "Capricornicus?" – Ally]

6. "Find out who his favourite football player is, and tell him that's your cousin. Course, this will only work if the famous footballer *is* your cousin, otherwise you'll look like a nutter."

7. "Laugh a lot – boys like a girl with a sense of humour. But don't do this if you're standing on your own, as you will look like a nutter. Again."

8. "Send him a psychic message that you like him. You'll know he's received it if you suddenly catch him staring at you."

[Check for gorgeous girls standing right behind you before you get excited, though – Ally]

9. "Wear a tonne of foundation on your face when you talk to him so he doesn't spot you blushing like an embarrassed tomato..."
[Is this bit of advice directed at me, Kyra? – Ally]

10. "...or grow a chin-length fringe. Sorted!"
[Very funny, *not*, Kyra Davies!]

the awesomeness of

Ah, Alfie. How cool art thou? Let me count the ways...

Your face. Everyone's got one, but yours is ... yum. It's all kind of skinny and pointy. (Er, I'm making you sound like a whippet, aren't I?) But you are indeed truly gorgeous, exactly like a young, groovy Brad Pitt. And luckily for me, you live in Crouch End and not Hollywood. (Phew.)

Your cute gold tooth. It's tucked away at the back, but I catch a glimpse of it twinkling when you're grinning. Oh, to be your dentist and spend so much time so close to those lips (and fillings).

Your very existence on the planet. My idea of hell would be a world without Alfie... Oh, and crisps. A world without crisps would be torture!

Your laid-backness. Yes, oh wondrous Alfie, I know that's not a proper word. But don't you see how perfect we could be together? You, with your (ahem) laid-backness, and me with my worriedness? It would be like yin and yang. ("Or ping and pong," Kyra has just said, but I'm ignoring her.)

Your eyes. You have two of them; they are both lovely. I wish I could stare into them, but that just makes me go wibbly and I have to look away very quickly, while blushing like a dork. It would be amazingly amazing if you gazed at me adoringly with those eyes, but sadly, you suffered a mental breakdown and chose to adore my sister Rowan instead of me. (Big swizz.)

Your smile. It could melt all the ice at the North Pole, if it wasn't already melting due to global warming.

Your leather bracelet. Ever since I've known you, you've worn that faded, worn string of brown leather tied around your wrist, like it's your special lucky charm. Kyra says it's skanky and probably smells, but what does *she* know.

SNOGGING:
a beginner's guide

Not exactly being an expert at this (like you didn't know!) I've enlisted some help...

Jen says: "The first time you kiss, everyone worries about where your nose is meant to go, but apparently 95% of people tilt their heads to the right, so you'll be OK. Unless you end up kissing one of the 5% of people who tilt to the left, I guess…"

Right? Left

Sandie says: "I think shy boys make the best kissers. The first boy I kissed was so shy, he said 'thank you' afterwards. Isn't that sweet?*" [*Er, no … 'cause I know for a fact that the first boy Sandie ever kissed was Billy. Blee! Talk about too much information! – Ally]

Kyra says: "French kissing is ace. Tongues rule! What do you mean, 'gross!', Ally?"

Kellie says: "If you do something dumb like clash teeth together, then just say oops! and kiss each other again straight away, before anyone's got time to get embarrassed!"

BRAd pITT

Chloe says: "Wear flavoured lip balm – he'll taste your strawberry kisses on his lips ages after you've gone!"

Salma says: "If you think someone's going to kiss you then you should stay as still as possible. Ally.*" [*Enough of the digs, Salma – how was I supposed to know for sure that Feargal O'Leary was trying to kiss me that time? And I didn't *mean* to crack his tooth when I leant over… – Ally]

Billy says: "I never used to know whether you were meant to suck or blow when you kissed someone. I found out that you're not meant to do either after I tried both out on the first girl I kissed. I got the message when she said, 'Yuck!', and then, 'What are you doing, you freak?!'"

Ally says: "Never kiss someone when you've just eaten. Tasting someone's tuna roll second-hand is about as romantic as getting your head trapped in a vice."

BILLY'S WORLD*

* Yep! Ally's let me write my very own bit! (Only she made me promise not to be "boring" about computer games or skateboarding...)

ABOUT MEEEEE!

• **My family** My dad is an insurance, um, something, and he likes reading the paper and pretending to be asleep when my mum is talking to him. My mum works in a big store and sells boring clothes to boring women and likes everything very, very neat. Her favourite invention ever is coasters. If you put a mug down on the table in our house and don't use a coaster you might as well turn yourself in to the police straight away. My big sister Beth lives in Paris, which is fine 'cause she thinks I'm as annoying as diarrhoea. We also have a poodle called Precious, who is sometimes yappy and annoying but that's 'cause he's embarrassed at his name and the state of his poncy haircut (Mum's choice). I'd like to let his fur grow into Rasta dreadlocks and call him Bob, after Bob Marley. I bet he'd be a really chilled-out dog then.

• **My friends**
My best mates are Hassan and Stevie, and sometimes Richie, when he isn't being a total big-headed pillock (so he isn't my mate very often, ha, ha, ha!). But my absolute best mate is Ally – we have been friends since we were really little kids. I can hang out and have fun with her just like I can with Stevie and Hassan, but the difference is, when I have a problem, I can talk to her about it. She always comes up with top ways to sort stuff out. Once she stops laughing at me, of course.

• **My school** It's called Muswell School for Boys and it is for boys only (duh!) which is really, really *booooorrrrrrrrrrriiinnnnggggg*. The only females at our school are some grouchy teachers (and Mrs Cameron has a moustache anyway), and the dinner ladies, who might make really good pizzas and spag bol but are unfanciable because they are about 110 years old and wear funny hairnets under their hats.

ACE!! things i Like doing

- **Skateboarding** [Soz – Ally's banned me from saying anything about this…]

- **Wearing baseball caps** I have 24 different baseball caps and they are all v cool. I would have 25 but the one my dad gave me – with "L&G Insurance" on it – does not count. I use it to stop the wonky leg on my desk from wobbling.

- **Listening to the Red Hot Chili Peppers** They are *soooo* cool.

- **Playing computer games** [Not allowed to talk about this. Swizz.)

- **Biscuit-cramming competitions** You've got to shove as many as you can in your mouth in one go without gagging.

- **Cycling fast downhill** (no brakes, natch!) Brilliant! Unless you hit a rock, of course.

- **Hanging out at Ally Pally** It's cool – there's the boating lake (fell in that a couple of times, ha!) and you can play football there and skateboard on the half-pipe by the ice rink and it's got great hills to cycle down.

Me and Ally meet there to walk our dogs, which is ace fun except when you have to pick their poo up in a plastic bag (minging).

- **Hanging out at Ally's house** Everything in Ally's house is kind of mental. The walls are painted mad colours, and loads of things don't work and they don't have a computer or anything but it doesn't matter. There are all these crazy animals and Ally's mum is lovely and thinks it's funny when I show her how many Jaffa Cakes I can put in my mouth in one go and doesn't freak out if I don't use a coaster.

WHY bOYS RULE!!!!!

'Cause they DO!!!
[Billy, that is totally pathetic… – Ally]

HOW WELL DO YOU KNOW

ALLY'S WORLD...?

IN BOOK 11

What's the shop in St Ives called where Ally's mum worked?

Is it

a. Seaweed Ceramics

b. Seabird Ceramics

c. Seafood Ceramics

IN BOOK 12

What does Ally say to one of the French boys to complete The Dare?

Is it

a. *J'ai treize ans et j'habite à Londres*
   (I'm thirteen and I live in London)

b. *Tu sais qu'elle a déjà un copain*
   (she has a boyfriend, you know)

c. *Je ne t'ai pas reconnu sans tes vêtements*
   (I didn't recognize you without your clothes)

ETCETERA

etcetera*

OK, so now you know (practically) everything about my family and my friends and stuff, but there are plenty of other things that are important to me (like food) or spook me (like dreams) or inspire me (like writing songs) so this next section is full of that kind of gubbins**. Hope it's as much fun for you to read as it was for me to write. (But hey, don't sue me if it's not.)

DANGER TOXIC

ETC

TOP LOVE SONG

* A more exciting way of saying "other stuff".
** A different way of saying "stuff".

(Mini) Contents

Yes, it's a potato!

MUM'S GALLERY

Here're some of **Mum's** hand-made works of art,
plus the names she's given them. (Note: sometimes
it's easier to work out what they are if you
squint a bit when you look at them.)

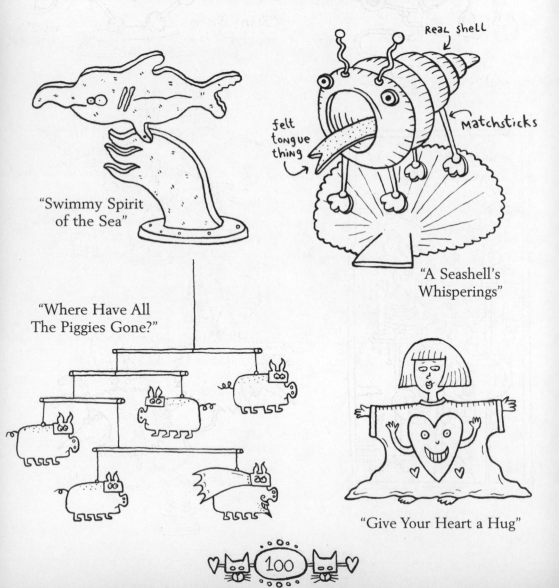

REAL shell

felt tongue thing

Matchsticks

"Swimmy Spirit of the Sea"

"A Seashell's Whisperings"

"Where Have All The Piggies Gone?"

"Give Your Heart a Hug"

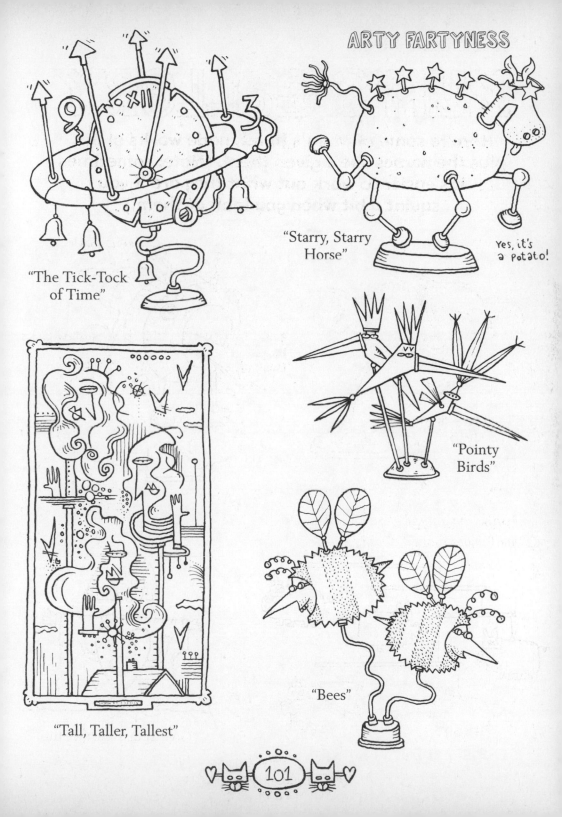

"The Tick-Tock of Time"

"Starry, Starry Horse"

Yes, it's a potato!

"Pointy Birds"

"Tall, Taller, Tallest"

"Bees"

ARTY FARTYNESS
JOIN-the-dots!

Tor wanted me to put this in. In case you need a clue, it's an animal (duh!).

Oops! I think Ivy might just have ruined it for you...

GLaM UP ON the cheap

Want to look good/interesting/unique? Got not much/no cash? I might just have a few ideas for you, with a little help from Rowan (uh-oh)...

What YOU'LL NEED

You should be able to find all the stuff below either lurking around the house or in charity shops (i.e. it should cost between zero pence and hardly anything).

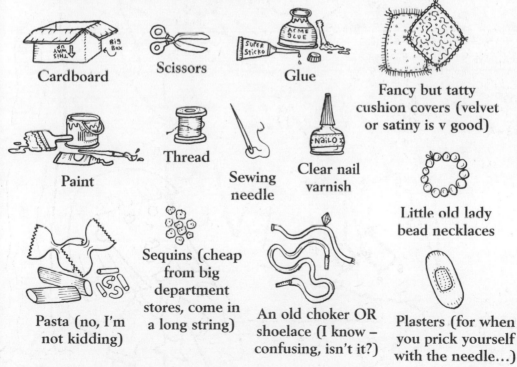

Cardboard

Scissors

Glue

Fancy but tatty cushion covers (velvet or satiny is v good)

Paint

Thread

Sewing needle

Clear nail varnish

Little old lady bead necklaces

Pasta (no, I'm not kidding)

Sequins (cheap from big department stores, come in a long string)

An old choker OR shoelace (I know – confusing, isn't it?)

Plasters (for when you prick yourself with the needle...)

And now for the clever part...
(TIP: you have to turn the page over first.)

We'd like to interrupt the clever part to bring you a special gift...
iT'S page 104
LOVELY STICKERS

ARTY FARTYNESS

CUTE CLIP

Paint a teeny-weeny butterfly on a bit of cardboard, then brush over with clear nail varnish when it's dry. Cut out and glue on to a plain hairclip.

SEEING STARS

Jazz up an old, plain T-shirt by stitching on a string of sequins in a star shape.

BEADY BAG

Chunky, old-fashioned bead necklaces might not look too hot round your neck, but they can be pretty groovy if you stitch them on to a boring bag.

Eat-Me Choker

First, get an old choker-length
necklace that you're bored
with, and take off whatever's
dangling from it now. (You
could use a plain black
shoelace too, or a piece
of ribbon.) Next get a
tube-shaped bit of pasta
(macaroni is good if you
want to be tasteful, or

penne if you want to make more of a statement).
Paint the pasta whatever colour/design you like, brush
over with clear nail varnish, and slide it on to your choker.

Petal Patches

Cut flower shapes out of
non-trashed parts of old
cushion covers, and stitch
on to jeans you've got
bored with.

PERMANENT SUNSHINE CUT FROM SHEET OF COLOURED PLASTIC.

MACARONI MOSAIC.

EL PARADISO

EXECUTIVE POPCORN DISPENSER.

*Blame Rowan if you think any/all of this is insane.

ALLY'S guide to Eating

Open mouth, insert crisp.
That's all there is to it, right?

Well, no – there's a whole exciting world of food out there, and it comes in all shapes, sizes and flavours. Some of it is brilliant (i.e. anything made by Grandma or Pizza Hut), and some of it is terrible (anything made by Rowan).

Grandma's cooking is great, mainly because she's got a thing for TV chefs (she's got a crush on "that nice Jamie Oliver") and copies everything off them, then tries their recipes out on us – hurrah! Mum's quite good too, although the stuff she makes tends to be a bit HH&G: (healthy, hippy and green). Dad's style is more OOAP: (out of a packet) but he always makes enough to feed a small nation so that's all right.

As for my sisters: Linn's a pretty good cook (she takes after Grandma, in more ways than one), Rowan's atrocious (see page 112 for examples), and my efforts are just extraordinary(-ly boring, see below). Tor and Ivy don't cook – they just eat (or make food art, see page 114).

Anyway, the next five pages will tell you all you never needed to know about food…

ALLY'S TOP TEA
A family favourite, guaranteed to please!
(For more recipes – edible and otherwise – see page 112…)

Ingredients:
Beans (3 tins)
Fish Fingers (3 packets)

Method:
Open tins of beans and empty into a pan. Heat. Meanwhile, put fish fingers under the grill, counting them to make sure none have been pinched by cunning pets with large appetites.
Check to see that beans and fish fingers are heated to correct temperature (i.e. if you stick your finger in the beans and end up yelping "Yeooow!", they are too hot). Next, shout "Oi! Tea's ready!", and "Rolf – leave those fish fingers alone!" and serve.

GRANDMA'S GUIDE TO NUTRITION

I asked Grandma to tell me what important vitamins and minerals are to be found in my favourite foods...

Nachos: "Ally, dear, nachos are hardly what I'd call nutritious."

Ready Salted crisps: "These must have as many vitamins and minerals as cardboard.*"

Bombay mix: "Deep-fried noodles and dried-out peas. I don't know what you're licking your lips for, Ally, but you're not likely to find a vitamin here!"

Milky Way Magic Stars: "Now you're just being silly."

Anything with a "Property of Linn Love" sticker on it:** "Well, if it's Linn's, it's bound to be healthy. But I don't think it's very nice to steal your sister's food, do you, Ally?"

* Actually, Grandma, that's not entirely true. For a start, salt is a mineral, right? And looking at the contents list of the packet of Ready Salted crisps I'm now eating, there is 2.2g of protein in there. According to my Biology teacher, the recommended daily intake of protein for a girl my age is 46g, so by *my* calculations, I need to eat 21 packets of crisps every day to hit that target! OK, so I'd end up looking like a human barrel on legs, but boy would I be healthy!

** See below.

"PROPERTY OF LINN LOVE"

Linn's amazing, she really is. She manages to buy herself these delicious treats that are both a) yummy and b) healthy. Just so that everyone knows to keep their hands off, she slaps these yellow stickers all over her stuff. Sadly for Linn, Rowan and me suffer from occasional temporary dyslexia, and instead of reading "Property of Linn Love", we see "Please eat me". Weird, that, isn't it?

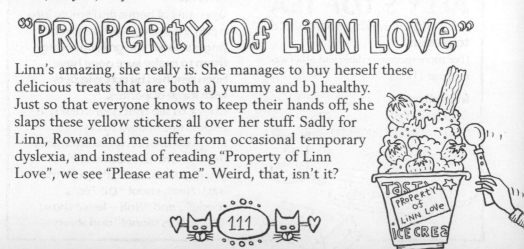

Café Rowan

MENU

Here at Café Rowan, we aim to give your tastebuds a shock.
Er, sorry – we meant a treat.

STARTERS

PICKLED CHICKEN NOODLE SOUP
Can of chicken noodle soup with a handful
of pickled onions chucked in

CURRIED LETTUCE SOUP, WITH CRISPY CROUTONS
Boiled lettuce, pinch of curry powder,
scrunched-up crisps sprinkled on top

SAUSAGE SOUP
Er, a sausage floating in some soup

MAIN COURSE

THREE "B"s OMELETTE

Fluffy omelette made with baked beans, broccoli and beetroot, served with a side order of Hula Hoops

FISHY RICE GLOOP

Sardines and rice in a rich tomato soup, lightly spiced with an Oxo cube and served with melted Dairylea triangles

PASTA SALAD À LA ROWAN

Half a tin of macaroni cheese, with a garnish of sweetcorn and raisins, on a bed of unboiled lettuce

PUDDINGS

BANANA SPLIT SURPRISE

The surprise is, it's an apple instead of a banana! The halved apple is topped with a dollop of jam, and drizzled with Cadbury's Chocolate Buttons

ROWAN'S RED HOT JELLY

Made entirely of red stuff; can you spot the raspberries, cherries and tomatoes floating in this delicious strawberry jelly?

CRUNCHY CUSTARD

What makes this mouthwatering custard so mysteriously crunchy? It's a secret ingredient only Chef Rowan knows! Comes with a sick-bucket

Coffee and indigestion tablets are on the house...

TOR'S FOOD ART

Our little brother's never had a hot meal in his life – mainly 'cause his food tends to go cold by the time he's "shaped" it into something artistic...

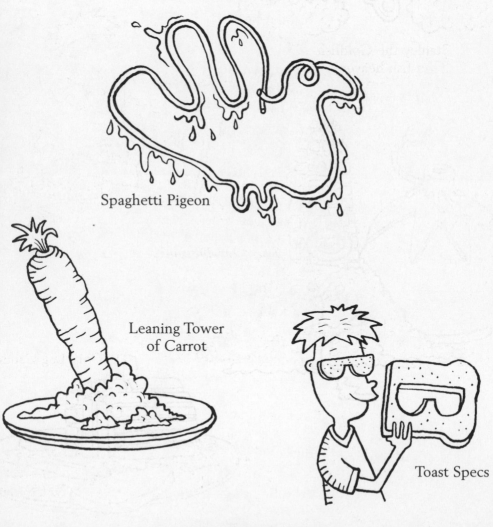

Spaghetti Pigeon

Leaning Tower
of Carrot

Toast Specs

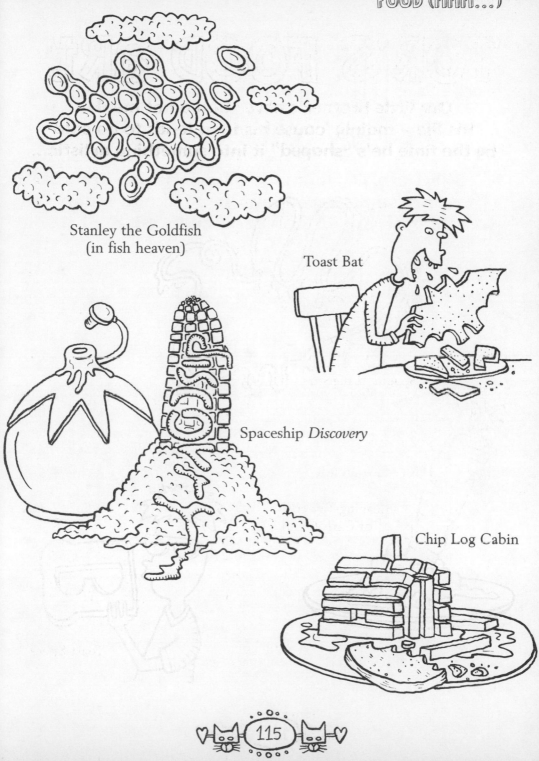

Stanley the Goldfish
(in fish heaven)

Toast Bat

Spaceship *Discovery*

Chip Log Cabin

BILLY'S Sandwich bar

It's Billy here. My mum likes buying posh bread. These are some top sandwiches I like to make with posh bread. (I'm dead cultured, me.)

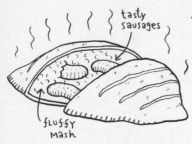

tasty sausages

fluffy mash

The Pitta Pocket
Pitta bread comes from Turkey and Greece. It's dead thin and flat but v cool, 'cause when you cut it in half you can open the bread up like a pocket and ram lots of stuff in it. Try sausage and mash.

The Crispy Ciabatta
Ciabatta is Italian. It looks kind of knobbly. Cut it in half, spread with some margarine, then empty a bag of crisps on it. (Any flavour will do.) Squirt with ketchup, if you fancy.

KETCHUP

CRISPS & ketchup... YUMMY!

The Cheesy Foccacia
Focaccia is Italian too. It's sort of flat-looking, like it was trying to be a ciabatta but then deflated. Cut open bread and spread some mustard on. Then unwrap an individual slice of cheese (mmm, my favourite kind!) and slap it in there. Spread more mustard on top, and repeat, till whole packet of cheese is used up and your mum's shouting at you 'cause it was meant to do for the entire week.

Week's SUPPLY of cheese

MUSTARD

spam, spam, spam, soy sauce & spam.

The Ooh-la-la French Stick

French sticks come from Kazakhstan. Ha! No, course they come from France. And Spam, well Spam comes from a tin, and it's like corned beef (ish). In fact it's very like corned beef, but it has a funnier name so I like it better. Anyway, spread loads of Spam on a French stick, and – here comes the Ooh-la-la part – add oriental seasoning, i.e. soy sauce. Eat fast, before the soy sauce makes the bread go soggy.

The Bananarama Naan

Naan bread is from India and it is *huuuuuugggggge*. It looks like a mutant pizza base. It's hard to cut open, so the best thing to do is smother it in peanut butter and chunks of banana and M&Ms (secret ingredient!) and then roll it up like a carpet and eat it.

BILLY'S INTERPRETATION OF ESSENTIAL FOOD TERMS

"Take-away" Heaven.

"Deep-pan" Delicious.

"Korma" Indian for delicious.

"Comes with chips" Brilliant.

"30% extra free" Excellent. (Especially on the top of a packet of Quavers.)

✂ - Cut out and keep

banish your inner SLOB

Sprawling on the sofa in your jim-jams with a cake may be as close to heaven as you can get, but (here comes the big swizz) it isn't actually a way of keeping fit. So here's my guide to top ways to exercise, as demonstrated by me and my mates...

SWIMMING
Good points: works lots of different muscles gently.
Bad points: swimming caps (the least flattering thing in the cosmiverse) and boys running into the Ladies' changing room 'cause their mates dared them to.

AEROBICS
Good points: gets your heart and lungs working hard (a good thing, apparently).
Bad points: star jumps. You just look like a dork.

KICK-BOXING
Good points: tough work-out. Gets rid of aggression.
Bad points: you pull some very scary faces.

YOGA
Good points: makes you very supple and relaxed. And bendy.
Bad points: getting stuck.

JOGGING
Good points: you get to exercise in the fresh air.
Bad points: makes your boobs jiggle.

BELLY-DANCING
Good points: it's a fun way to exercise.
Bad points: shaking your bum at high speeds can feel very, very silly.

DOG-WALKING
Good points: doesn't feel like exercise, and you can gossip with mates while you're doing it.
Bad points: scooping poop.

HOW TO DO

Putting make-up on properly is tricky and I should know, considering I've gone out looking a right state sometimes. But here're some tips from Linn on how it should be done.

Blusher
"Dust blusher on to the apples of the cheeks using a circular motion. Aim for a smaller circle than this."

Lipstick
"Lipgloss is easier, but if you want to use lipstick, the golden rule is to follow your lipline, rather than just making a funny shape, Ivy."

Beauty spot
"In a spot emergency, you can hide the pesky zit by dotting on some brown eyeliner pencil to create a beauty spot. This is only convincing when it's covering one spot, though."

Make-Up

WORDS: LINN. MAKE-UP: IVY. MODEL: BILLY.

Mascara

"The look you're aiming for is natural, instead of a spider that's been stood on. And ideally, mascara should be worn on the eyelashes, and not the forehead."

Eyeshadow

"For best results, apply a light dusting of eyeshadow at the corners of each eye (no, Ivy, the outside corners), using a brush, rather than a thumb."

Note from Billy:
Ally blackmailed me into doing this. Well, OK, it was more of a dare. We were playing Truth or Dare and I chose Dare. Doh! Wish I'd gone for Truth now. I mean, how embarrassing would it have been to admit that the longest I've worn a pair of socks without changing them was a week and a half? Erm…

TOR'S guide to GROOMING

For some strange reason, my little brother is dying to contribute some top hairdressing tips for this page. Take it away, Tor! (This should be interesting…)

"Brushing hair is important. It is important because if you are moulting and lick your hair instead of brushing it, you will sick up a hairball. Specially if you eat some grass too. Don't know why."

[Thank you for that, Tor! I'm sure that will come in very handy if any of us are reincarnated as a cat – Ally]

HOW to Write a LOVE SONG (ha!)

**Fancy writing your own slushy-gushy love song?
Hope your first attempt is better than mine...**

Me and my sister Rowan once wrote a song – it was for her mate Chazza's band. "Wow – you wrote an *actual* song, that an *actual* band played?!" I hear you cry? (Well, I don't really, but you get my drift.) What I'm trying to say is that writing a song might sound kind of impressive, but it's not like me and Ro just sat down and the words all flowed *magically* on to the paper. Oh no. It took loads of attempts (most of them rubbish) and we used up loads of paper (most of it ending up in scrunched balls in the bin) before we got something half-decent.

And that half-decent thing was called "Not Enough"*. Just to give you an idea of how tough it was to write this song, I have to let you know that when we first started out, it was called "You Give Me The Wibbles" (see right). That was until we decided that "You Give Me The Wibbles" sounded about as romantic as someone giving you a Chinese burn. And it didn't help that Tor wandered in and saw the title and asked if the wibbles was a kind of disease, like measles or athlete's foot or something.

Anyway, just in case any of you fancy giving song-writing a go, here's a sneak preview of our original lyrics, plus the ones we ended up with. Thought it might help cheer you up if you get stuck...

* Rowan doesn't know, but I secretly wrote the words for Alfie. Oh, the shame if anyone found out!

(Er, if I didn't want anyone to find out then maybe it was a dumb idea to have written that down here...)

"Not enough"

"You Give Me The Wibbles" by Ally and Rowan Love

You smile, but it makes me ~~wibble~~ shiver,

You look my way and it makes me ~~barf~~ shake,

Ever time you talk to me

I'm sure it's just some mistake.
~~I think you're just having a laugh.~~

There's no point to ~~fancying you~~ loving you rotten,

There's no point in ~~my heart going ping!~~ all this pain,

There's no way ~~you could fancy a dork like me~~ this is going to happen,

Why put myself through it again and again?
~~So who am I kid-ding?~~

People say love is special,

But I think love ~~sucks big-time~~ is tough,

'Cause I know you like me,
~~And I don't know how to finish this stupid song,~~

Just not enough,
~~'Cause I can't think of anything to rhyme,~~

Not enough,
~~Rhyme,~~

Not enough.
~~Rhyme...~~

What DREAMS mean (maybe)

As an experiment, I asked my family what they dreamt about last night, and looked up meanings in a book I got out of the library. Then I ignored what it said and interpreted their dreams myself...

Mum's dream: "There was this gorgeous parakeet soaring up in a blue sky."
The Dream book says: "Both the sky and birds represent freedom."
Ally's interpretation: My mum is lovely, but a bit of a bird-brain.

Dad's dream: "Someone kept asking me these dumb questions about dreams, and then I went deaf!"

The Dream book says: "Deafness means closing your ears to the truth."
Ally's interpretation: My dad is pulling my leg.

Linn's dream: "I dreamt I was doing my homework." **The Dream book says:** "Working relentlessly equals a desire for control." **Ally's interpretation:** Linn needs to have *way* more fun.

Tor's dream: "I was stroking lots of hamsters." **The Dream book says:** "Dreaming of hamsters indicates no direct goal." **Ally's interpretation:** Tor has a goal all right: to stroke every hamster he can get his hands on.

Rowan's dream: "There was this Barbie doll, and she came alive and then asked me the way to Woolworth's!" **The Dream book says:** Too weird even for the weird dream book. **Ally's interpretation:** My sister is insane.

Ivy's dream: "There was balloons!" **The Dream book says:** "You are at the mercy of the winds of change." **Ally's interpretation:** More like, they had a party at her nursery yesterday and there were lots of balloons. (See how easy this dream interpretation lark is?)

DO WHAT I SAY AND YOUR LIFE WON'T SUCK

Excellent things that'll brighten up your day, your week, your life. (I hope!)

1. Write the good stuff down. You don't have to keep a diary – or a journal like I do – but scribble all the nice things that happen to you in a day in a little notebook (a cute guy smiled at you from a bus/you miraculously passed your maths test/you found a pound coin in the street/your fringe didn't sit stupid for once). When you're having a blue day, it's great to look back and see that plenty of good stuff happens to you too.

2. Tell people you like that you like them. Everyone likes compliments, and if you get one, you're more likely to give them back – yesss!

3. Stop moaning about the bits of you that you don't like. Christina Aguilera once warbled on about believing you're beautiful. Well personally, I find that hard to take seriously, but telling yourself "You aren't that bad, y'know, in every single way" sounds easy enough.

4. Start appreciating the bits of you that are OK! See above. And I have quite pretty feet, so there.

5. Sniff flowers. They're cool. And they smell heaps better than poncy, fancy perfumes.

6. Always stop and pat cats in the street. Makes you feel good – don't know why. (Maybe they should do scientific tests on it. I'll mention it to Miss Kyriacou next time I'm in her class…)

7. Smile at dogs in the street. Ditto.

8. Tidy your room. Go on, admit it – it feels much better when the floor's visible.

9. Tickle a friend. Why does tickling someone else make you laugh? (I'd better get Miss Kyriacou on to that, too.)

10. Get your own back on scary people (safely). Imagine them sitting on the loo. I used to do that with Mrs Fisher, our horrible year head; she was a lot less scary after that.

11. Just when you're about to be bitchy about someone, shut up. Must get Kyra and Chloe to read this one.

12. Never pass a grassy hill without rolling down it. Living right next door to Alexandra Palace means I've done a lot of rolling in my time.

13. Eat something you've never tried before. I don't mean worms, or anything Rowan's cooked; I mean stuff like olives or Marmite or weird fish. It could end up being your favourite food ever.

14. Take up blowing bubbles as a hobby. Why should little kids have all the fun?

15. Be nice to your mum. As someone whose mum wasn't around for a long, long time, trust me when I say you'd miss her if she wasn't there.

16. Don't be friends with someone who doesn't deserve you. Kyra had to work pretty hard to prove she could be a decent mate. (Even if there are still times when I could cheerfully strangle her.)

17. Enjoy stuff, even if you're rubbish at it. You don't have to be good at something to get a kick out of it. Look at Billy and skateboarding!

18. Sing! Feels great to do, even if (like Rowan) you should only do it in a soundproofed booth.

19. Dance! Do it every chance you get, including round the house. Don't worry about scaring cats/dogs/small brothers or sisters. In fact, get them to join in.

20. Look in the mirror every morning and tell yourself that your life doesn't suck. Just do it!

OK, that's all from me and my world, but there's just time to find out more about a couple of people who helped me with this book...

Karen's (mini) Nosey Questionnaire

Name: Karen McCombie (middle name Grace, if you want to get picky).

Nickname: Mrs McCrumble.

Job: Writing words, in between eating crisps, patting cats and cooing over Spike's drawings.

My favourite flavour of crisp is: Tomato sauce (this week).

Do I have anything small and furry living in my house?: I have three small furry cat-shaped things; Cecy (female, black and white, old, grumpy, sharp), and Gus and Bysshe (twin brothers, fat, ginger, thick). There is also a big, non-furry person in the house; he is called Tom (husband, human cushion to Cecy).

Favourite way to waste time: Belly dancing, and frightening the cats with all the tinkling.

What's my deepest, darkest secret?: I love Brussels sprouts.

If I could spend a day in Ally's world I'd...: Cuddle Rolf, snog Billy, put a wrinkle in Linn's duvet cover and try on all Rowan's clothes.

brain full of plots, stupid stuff and cat hair

KM°C

Spike's (mini) Nosey Questionnaire

Name: Spike Gerrell

Nickname: Er ... Spike. Actually, my real name is Simon, but Spike seems to have taken over.

Job: Drawing pictures for a living has got to be one of the best jobs ever!

My favourite flavour of crisp is: Plain, Ready Salted or Salt 'n' Shake ... always has been. (Wish I'd put tomato sauce flavour, like Karen. Plain sounds a bit, er, plain.)

Do I have anything small and furry living in my house?: Willard the fat striped cat has ruled our house since time began. However, our new lovely baby boy Ethan (small but not furry) is starting to take over. Girlfriend Kaz tries to keep control of all of us.

Favourite way to waste time: Easy! Playing with Ethan, playing football ... looking forward to being able to play football with Ethan.

What's my deepest, darkest secret?: I think I'd secretly like to be Tor!

If I could spend a day in Ally's world I'd...: Try to buy the house next door to Ally's 'cause then I could visit all the time and hang out with the cool and groovy Rowan and help Tor look after all his pets.

brain full of pictures, football and cat hair

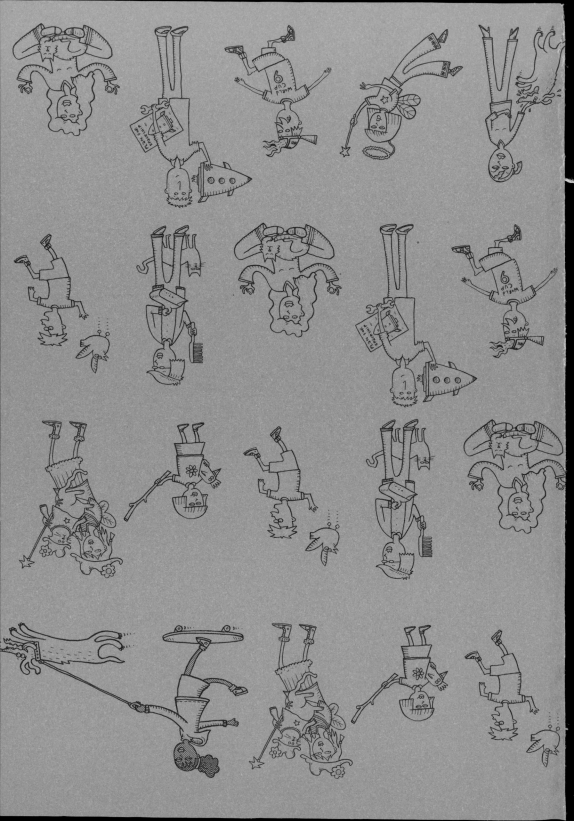